Reviews for
Trading Ashes for Beauty

What a great read! In this, his first novel, Rick Clendenen introduces the reader to Chuck Haynes, a man who has just experienced the tragic loss of his closest friend and mentor. Rick compellingly writes about Chuck's journey from his grief and isolation back to the place of one determined to serve others and fully engage in God's purpose for his life. Along the way, Chuck learns the importance and value of relationships and spiritual life lessons everyone needs to learn.

Dr. Donnie Peal
Executive Director ORU Educational Fellowship
Tulsa, Oklahoma

Trading Ashes for Beauty is deeply moving and penetrates into the roots of human behavior. It is so emotionally and spiritually moving, that everyone can find true meaning.

Jessica Ford
English Teacher
North Laurel High School
London, Kentucky

It was our honor to read the pages of the first draft of *Trading Ashes for Beauty* with Rick and Debbie. The way in which Rick wove God's Word and His plan for the lives of the characters was intriguing. Each chapter left us anxious for the next. The characters were true to life and we felt as if they were a part of our own family. The book brought tears as we delved into the intimate lives of each character.

Roy and Cheryl Hodges
Business Leaders/Entrepreneurs
Paducah, Kentucky

BOOK I
THE JOURNAL SERIES

TRADING

ASHES FOR

Beauty

A Journey from Tragedy to Triumph

RICK CLENDENEN

Trading Ashes for Beauty, *A Journey from Tragedy to Triumph*
Book 1, The Journal series
by Rick Clendenen

First Print Edition, September 2016
ISBN-13: 978-1539034360
ISBN-10: 1539034364

Cover Art: "Ashes to Beauty" by Katie Joh
Cover and interior design by Suzanne Fyhrie Parrott

Order additional copies of this book and other resources
by Rick Clendenen online at: www.rcminc.org

or contact Rick Clendenen at

Rick Clendenen Ministries
PO Box 287
Benton, KY 42025
Office: (606) 848-1495

Please provide feedback

Dedication

I'm at the stage in my life now that when I bend over to pick up something from the floor, I pause to ask myself if there is anything else I need while I am down there. I think you understand my situation.

Yet, recently I found myself sitting flat on the kitchen floor, looking straight across into the beautiful blue eyes of my granddaughter. What on earth could bring an old man down to such an uncomfortable position? The culprit was Playdoh. Little did I realize that when I bought it for her, I would be forced to demonstrate my skill level. Of course, it didn't take long for me to make a yellow snake with red eyes and a red forked tongue. I must admit that she was not impressed with my artistic ability! Yet, one thing remains fixed in my mind from that experience—it was seeing my fingerprints in the Playdoh and realizing that I was fingerprinting her life as well.

This book is a tribute to three men that have left their fingerprints in my life as they have spent countless hours in uncomfortable positions, shaping my character, forming my integrity, and redefining my personality. Everywhere I look, I see their fingerprints and it causes me to wonder what shape I would be in today without their touch in my life.

I write these words with the deepest of love, admiration, and respect for Dr. John Thomas Parish, Dr. Dale Yerton, and Pastor Richard Dale Clendenen, Jr. These are three men that have marked my life forever. Thank you!

Acknowledgements

Life, for me, is like a circus where many times I find myself in the center ring of a packed tent with lights glaring in my eyes while people are watching what I will do next while I, on the other hand, stand clueless. Yet, every time I think it's all over, God faithfully steps in and, by His mercy, rescues me from imminent destruction.

I have so many people to thank for this project but number one, I want to thank my Lord and Saviour, Jesus Christ who has made it all possible by directing the right people into my life at the right time to distract the crowd's attention and to direct my next step toward my destiny. He's not a part of my life, He's all my life.

Then, of course, there's my friend, Tom Watkins, whose fascination with gold has not only set the course for his life but has been instrumental in educating me for the writing of this book. Your knowledge and patience is much appreciated.

There are my assistants. Dr. Jose Bonilla-my book agent and lifelong friend that is always willing to do whatever job is necessary to make my story become a reality. Words cannot describe my love and appreciation to you, my friend, for all that you do.

I want to thank Jessica Ford for making all the grammatical corrections. Thank you—you are a blessing! My sincere appreciation and thanks go to Kim Soesbee of Touch Publishing Services. Your expertise in the editing process was invaluable. My gratitude also goes to Suzanne Fyhrie Parrott for formatting and preparing this book for publication. I appreciate all your work!

And last, but not least, I want to thank Katie Joh for designing the beautiful cover and for being such a wonderful addition to the Clendenen family. Thank you!

What would a circus be without the clowns and my family has stepped in to fill the gap: my wife, my kids, my grandkids, and two very special friends, Roy and Cheryl Hodges who have made the journey with me. They've kept me laughing through the painstaking hours when I doubted whether or not I would finish and they have given me hope by believing in me. Thanks, guys. I wouldn't want to do life without any of you. You are my joy and this one is for us.

Introduction

If you were awakened tonight by your smoke detector to discover that your house was engulfed in flames and you had only five minutes to retrieve your most prized possessions, what would you be willing to risk your life for? Naturally, the answer is, your family. For everything else is just possessions and whether or not they could be replaced, they in no way equal the treasure of human relationships.

This question spawned the book you hold in your hands today. The older I get, the more I come to understand that the real treasures in life are people. In fact, each person is like a gold mine, waiting in the dark to be discovered and cherished if only you are willing to take the risk and put forth the effort necessary to retrieve them.

My honest prayer and desire for you is that while you read this novel, you will take a personal inventory of your life and commit yourself to take full advantage in developing lasting relationships. That, in doing so, you will discover just how wealthy you are. True prosperity is found in the things you possess that money cannot buy. Enjoy the journey.

Contents

Chapter 1

Let the Search Begin

The piercing sound of the alarm clock penetrated the darkness of an otherwise tranquil bedroom, announcing the end of a restless night and the beginning of a brand new day that was sure to be filled with new experiences. For me, it was the day to put into practice all that I had learned at the feet of Johnny Dale. I cut the alarm off, fumbling around in the darkness until my fingers found the light switch.

The details of the weekend, Johnny's death, his wake, and his funeral replayed in my mind as if they were a bad dream. I desperately wanted to banish them, but to no avail. Words from Johnny's own mouth spoke to the moment. I could hear him say, "Death is nothing more than a part of life." Yet death had laid claim to one of the greatest men I had ever known, leaving me with only the memories and the lessons he had taught me to maximize my life for God's glory. Johnny had been my mentor for over 20 years. "Where do I even begin to live my life without him?" I wondered aloud.

Padding to the kitchen, I poured myself a cup of coffee before reaching for my Bible and devotional, a daily habit that I formed on the very first day that we had met. I could hear Johnny's voice as if it were only yesterday, "The Bible is the foundation for your life and the roadmap for your future." Indeed, it had proven to be both.

I was stunned to see what God had in store for me. The title of this day's devotional simply read: Let the Search Begin. It was the story of a man who had, as a young child, been separated by war from his parents. As a man, he began to search for his family roots. His journey had led him through heartache, as well as great acts of heroism that had preserved his very life. He discovered that his family had given him away because they knew that he would not survive the trip they had to make as refugees. Their wisdom had proven true since all of them had been killed on the journey.

The search led him to discover the providence of God. He had not only survived, but in turn had given his life to Jesus Christ and was now the president of an organization dedicated to connecting others with their heritage. His story was one of triumph out of tragedy where God set the stage for future ministry. The devotional ended with Romans 8:28: For God really does work all things together for our good. It advised: The deeper we search this out, the more quickly we too will discover His plan for our life.

I knew in my soul it was now time for my search to begin.

With my devotion behind me and the day before me, I was ready to get started in carrying out my mission. I began by checking the gear, loading the truck, and making sure I had everything needed to accomplish the task. It was up to me. Johnny could no longer cover my mistakes or rescue me from another blunder. The time had come for me to step up and take my place. He had always assured me that when the time came, I would be ready to assume the responsibility. I must prove that his belief in me was not in vain.

With the truck packed, I checked the list for a final time: the lights, the battery, the water, the safety equipment, food, pick, shovel, screen, and pan. Everything was in place except my confidence, and I supposed that would come in due season. One thing was evident-how much I depended on him. After all, he was known as the gold prospector around these parts and I was a lot more comfortable being called his sidekick, a title I carried with pride as we had spent countless hours panning for gold in the abandoned mines of the Sierra Nevada Mountains.

As I jumped into the truck, I made a last quick call to my accountability partner, Jim, to tell him exactly where I would be.

Driving toward the mountain, my mind flooded with thoughts as the sun shone brightly in my face, each ray declaring hope for the future. As I made my way to the darkness, suddenly I remembered the story of Christ that Johnny had shared with me on our first trip this way. He talked about how Jesus had left the splendor of Heaven and invaded the darkness in search for us. He shared how it had inspired him to be a prospector. He knew that in the midst of the darkness lay nuggets of gold—lost and in need of someone to redeem them from the dirt. He talked about Romans 5:8 and how God commended His love toward us; that while we were yet sinners, Christ died for us. I could still see the tear in the corner of his eye as he glanced at me that day and said, "Chuck, we are the nuggets, hidden in the muck and the mire, lost in the darkness, with no hope of redemption without His intervention, yet He came to change our destiny once and for all. What a story! What a Savior!" The story worked and so did the Savior that day as I gave my life to Jesus Christ. I'd become a searcher myself to redeem lost treasures, both naturally and spiritually.

The trip flew by thanks to my wandering in the amazing grace of God. First things first, and the first thing was to put on my transponder, a signal to keep me from losing my way. One cannot ignore his own safety as he journeys into the darkness of a mine. Without a safety plan for recovery, you will surely find yourself in need of rescue. All of us can lose our way from time to time, and none of us are wise enough to predict the future. Behold, when you think you stand, take heed, lest you fall!

With a backpack in place and the wagon loaded, it was time. Putting on my hat and flipping down my light, I made my way toward the opening of the mine. The dampness under my feet contrasted the cool air which greeted my face as I encountered the gross darkness. I always take a moment to make adjustments. You cannot rush this process; you must acclimate to your new surroundings. I continued once fully satisfied that I was ready.

Mining is an unusual process where experience becomes your greatest teacher. Everything looks the same underground, but not every area will yield the same rewards. Sometimes the greatest yield comes from the most unlikely places. The wise prospector knows where to start and how to maximize his efforts. Of course, this is where Johnny would say, "And it doesn't hurt anything to pray, you know!" I agree, so I spoke out: "Lord, help me in this endeavor. You know my heart's desire as well as my pain. And you are able to do exceedingly, abundantly above all that I ask or think."

Always when mining, the farther I go down, the less comfortable I feel with the various sounds filling the air: the popping and cracking of the timbers; the continual dripping of water; and the host of critters and insects, chirping, clicking, and chattering. Distraction hinders focus and I must continually remind myself that these distinct noises are all just a part of the dig. I finally reached the place that Johnny frequently said offered the greatest promise. I unloaded the equipment and got to work.

Sparks flew with the first swing of the pick as I hit solid rock—a sure sign to change my action. I traced the rock with my finger to test its size. Only a few inches across in diameter, I worked to pry it loose with my fingers. This would be my entry point for the dig. Alternating from pick to shovel, one thing became abundantly clear from the start—there's a lot more of dirt and rock in this process than there is gold. But you are never going to find the gold if you're unwilling to work for it. With every shovelful, I allowed my light to scan the dirt, looking for just a glimmer, an indication, a promise of a nugget. Anything shining would be loaded on the wagon, the rest discarded to the side.

Minutes turned into hours. My labor continued. Thank God for my bandana, tied around my head to prevent the copious amounts of sweat from running into my eyes. Suddenly, the pick offered a different sound. Excitement filled my heart as the light on my helmet revealed the glitter of gold. The mother lode! With every swing of the pick, another nugget was revealed, erasing the pain of my previous labor. I imagine the feeling to be like the travailing mother's joy after giving birth to a child; pain replaced with thrill.

I stopped for a moment to look at my pocket watch. Two

o'clock. The day was quickly passing and I wondered, Do I dig on, or do I eat lunch and take a rest? Once again, the voice of Johnny gave an answer, "Sometimes the chips fly faster when you take time to sharpen the axe." In his quip I knew I had better calm my excitement down and refuel my body because I couldn't afford to run out of fuel later.

At a quarter till three I knew I had about three hours left before I needed to head home. I must utilize my time for maximum effect. Now that I'd found the seam of gold, every shovel turn produced more and more nuggets of every size. This had indeed been my most profitable day.

With the wagon full, I still had a little over two hours to filter this load. It would be tight, but doable. My lunch kicked in, and, with the adrenaline, I gained my second wind. I set up to filter the dirt through the screen at the entrance of the mine by the creek, a perfect spot. Little by little, moment by moment, the dirt gave up nuggets, each one bringing me closer to my (and Johnny's) purpose.

Yes, there was a purpose for our madness. Johnny and I had worked this project for over a year. Today's haul may have put us over the top in making our dream a reality. For us, it was never about the gold; it was about the purpose!

As the sun began to set behind the mountain, I dumped the last scoop of dirt into the filter, yielding more precious nuggets. I'm sure that good planning, proper management, and prayer had enabled me to reach my goal. It was time to load up and head home.

Everything looked different as I made my way back down the mountain. I could see the lights of several little towns scattered across the valley, each light made possible by the work of someone. I may never know their name, but the light somehow declared it simply by shining. I stopped by the Burger Shack to pick up supper, since I was much too tired to fix a meal and much too dirty to go in anywhere.

I took my precious bag of nuggets inside my home. Stopping at the utility room, I stripped off my dirty clothes and headed to a hot shower, setting the gold inside the washing machine for safe keeping. Cleaned up, I wandered back into the kitchen. There on the table was my Bible and devotional. I picked them both up and sat down in my recliner.

As I rocked back, I felt something under the right side of my chair. It was a journal that Johnny had bought for me. In fact, it was the last thing he had given me. He had encouraged me to record my thoughts, but to be honest, I'd never seen the need or purpose for journaling. Maybe this was the day to begin. My practice had always been to have devotion and prayer time in the morning and Bible reading at night. I'm sure I could add a few minutes at night to journal what the day had taught me.

On this evening, my reading was the fifteenth chapter of St. Luke's Gospel, the parable of the lost sheep, the lost coin, and the lost son. I smiled as I realized that I had been set up by the Holy Spirit once again. I picked up my journal and began to write, entitling the page Let the Search Begin. What I learned worth noting:

- Everyone needs redemption.
- Redemption is very costly.
- Redemption is the product of a labor of love.
- Redemption requires us to bring what is in darkness to light.
- The redemption process requires us to be secure ourselves.
- Redemption often goes unseen by others.
- Redemption is always worth the effort.

That wasn't as bad as I thought it would be, I mused. I guess I'll add the journal to my daily routine. It was time for bed, and I was exhausted. I used up my strength and only God knew what tomorrow would bring.

Chapter 2

Purification by Fire

As the sunrise struggled against the dense fog that blanketed our little valley in the morning, I realized the weatherman was right this time—visibility was zero! It'd been another restless night for me, left alone to battle with my thoughts; it felt as if the real fog was between my ears. The irony of Johnny's death had me in its grip, and the unanswered questions pried open the vault of memories that had been buried over two decades ago. They also challenged me to consider the possibility of a better future. As I pondered both, my heart began to race within me, as fear and anxiety yielded more questions without answers. I didn't understand why bad things happened to good people, especially when the good people were about doing the Master's business. Why did a great man like Johnny Dale have to die, while other people half his worth lived on in his absence? Only God will be able to answer that for me one day.

You see, Johnny Dale was the chief of the Fallon, Nevada Fire Department. I will never forget the first time we met. It was December 18, 1990. I was twenty-two years old; Susie and I had been married for three years. Our first Christmas with our daughter Lizzie was approaching. She would be turning one in January. Life could not have been better. We had gone all out on Christmas decorations since every light seemed to grab Lizzie's attention and filled her face with joy. I came home from work that night at 1:00 AM after working afternoons on swing shift at the FedEx Distribution Center in Carson City, Nevada. I was a forklift driver, and it was my job to load the trucks for the next day's delivery. I was blessed to have the job, and I had high seniority. The future looked bright with all kinds of opportunities for advancement.

I remember slipping into the house. Everything was quiet as I tiptoed down the hallway toward Lizzie's room. I noticed that Susie had fallen asleep in her attempt to get Lizzie into the bed, so I decided to leave them both there. They looked so peaceful, lying there asleep, Lizzie in her crib and Susie just an arm's length away. A smile crossed my face as I said to myself, I'm the luckiest man in all the world.

I made my way toward our bedroom to get some much needed rest. I paused for a moment, stared at the Christmas tree, and made my way around the presents that we had bought for Lizzie. Obviously we had gone completely overboard. And why not—she was our everything!

I fell asleep as soon as my head hit the pillow exhausted from a hard day at work. We were filling all the Christmas orders. I was soon awakened by a thick cloud of smoke. The fire alarm was declaring that something was tragically wrong! I jumped to my feet, realizing that I had forgotten to turn off the Christmas tree lights. Our entire living room was engulfed in flames! Immediately, I started screaming to the top of my lungs for Susie and Lizzie as I tried to make my way through the fire. That was the last thing I remembered.

The next scene is forever fixed in my memory as I stared in the face of Johnny Dale. He was straddling me, holding down both of my hands, assuring me that I would be OK. I couldn't speak for the oxygen mask that covered my face. With every ounce of strength, I was fighting to take it off and to get on my feet. He knew exactly why. I'll never forget, as tears rolled down his cheeks, he simply shook his head no.

A knot formed in the pit of my stomach and I knew they were gone. Gone forever; my world would never be the same. I may physically recover, but the void in my life would never be filled. It was all my fault. How would I ever be able to live with myself? How ironic that twenty years later, Johnny himself would die in a house fire trying to retrieve one of his men who found himself trapped trying to save another family in crisis. The house collapsed on them all.

What I had long-feared had come to pass. Johnny's compassion would often override his wisdom and he frequently put himself in harm's way to rescue others from dangerous situations. That, my friend, was Johnny Dale. No one could ever change that. Nor would they want to, since it was his compassion that made him so special.

For over twenty years, Johnny had really never let go of my hands. He had walked with me every step of my journey while making me a part of his family. I shudder to think of what I might have become had he not been in my life. Shirley and Johnny had their own share of trouble and so had JD. They had one son named Jonathan; he was married to Rebecca, and JD was their only grandchild and indeed, their pride and joy. When JD was just eighteen months old, Rebecca left him and Jonathan with nothing but a note and an empty bank account. Apparently she had found someone else and never planned to return. Jonathan tried to handle his pain through medication and soon found himself addicted. That led him to selling drugs to support his habit. Shirley and Johnny had attempted many times to get him into rehabilitation and felt that they had miserably failed. Jonathan experienced one drug bust after another until he landed in prison in Ely, Nevada where he is now serving twenty years without parole. All these events happened before JD turned six years old. Johnny and Shirley adopted him when he was seven. Now, only five years later, JD and Shirley are left alone at the most crucial time in this young man's life.

I knew I would step to the plate and make sure that Shirley and JD never lacked for anything as long as I lived. It's the least I could do for there was no way I could ever repay all that this family had done for me. In reality, I was scared to death. I could hear Johnny's strong voice clearly speaking to me from the past, reminding me, "It's the trying times that make us strong; for it's in our weakness His strength is made perfect. We can't even tap in to the strength of God until all our strength has been depleted."

Such truth! That's where I stood at that very moment, void of the answers I needed and uncertain of what questions to even ask. The only thing that remained secure was that God was able to see me through and that must be enough. As all those thoughts circled to a close, I knew I'd better get started with my day.

As I opened the bedroom door, the smell of fresh brewed coffee greeted me. Oh how I love my automated coffee pot! Just set the time and forget about it. It was a lot more scheduled than I was.

With a snack cake in one hand and coffee in the other, I made my way toward the recliner. I set down my coffee and picked up my devotional to see what the day held for me.

The devotion described an inventor and how he had spent most of his life looking for what was missing, rather than what was present. The void had given him multiple opportunities to create products for people who were sometimes unaware that they even needed them. He put every product he invented through rigorous testing, not to reveal its weakness, but to ensure its strength.

That spoke directly to me. We must realize that God never allows us to face struggles to prove how really weak we are, but rather, for the purpose of increasing our strength. He knows full well that the victories of today are what prepare us for the battles of tomorrow. We cannot endure without them.

It was time to get to work. I didn't have far to go, just across the back yard. Years ago, Johnny and I had built a block workshop that looked more like a bomb shelter, but we built it for the purpose of smelting gold. He insisted that we build it on my property. I believe his intent was to make sure that I would tie myself to the hobby that we had shared. He also insisted that we construct it out of block and plaster for these two reasons: the insulation factor and because both are fire retardants.

You see, in order to smelt gold, the temperature must reach 1,750 degrees Fahrenheit. You can't afford to let temperatures like that get away from you. Therefore, the building stood across the lot, away from every other structure, with all the safety precautions necessary, not only for our safety, but also with the safety of others in mind. Besides all that, I have to admit, it became quite a conversation piece in our neighborhood and I enjoyed making up stories about its true use. Of course, our neighbors eventually knew them all.

The fog lingered as I strode across my yard. A heavy dew hopped from the tips of the grass and onto my boots. I hoped the overcast skies would help me deal with the day's intense heat. I needed all the help I could get.

Unlocking the padlock from the front door, I flipped on the lights and started the process of lighting the fire. It's a lot more difficult than lighting a fireplace. The heat must be kept low but extremely intense. It would be sustained by a mixture of oxygen and fuel and must be lit with a blow torch. The cauldron itself was surrounded by red clay firebrick to assist me in keeping the fire at the correct temperature. On the rack sat a graphite pot, over half an inch thick. Its purpose was to hold the gold itself because the melting point for graphite is much higher than gold's. It took me a while to get everything ready; there are no shortcuts in the process. Patience is the key!

I soaked all the gold nuggets in Borax detergent to remove all excess mire from them. You see, the problem with gold is that it tries to stick to everything. This was an all-day process. The thermometer on the wall already read 115 degrees. The windows were open, as well as both doors, and the fan blew at full speed, but the sweat still rolled down my face. There was just no easy way to do this.

The time came to place the gold in the pot. I made sure that every nugget was completely dry, since water could split the pot wide open. The gauge showed 1600 degrees. It would take at least another hour before smelting would begin. Yet already, everything glowed cherry red and the heat radiating off the oven overwhelmed the room.

After loading the pot, I looked at my pocket watch. A quarter till twelve. Knowing I couldn't afford to skip my lunch, and also that I couldn't leave the situation unguarded, I had planned ahead and packed my lunch and water in a cooler. Hydration was vital, especially in this kind of heat. I took my seat outside the building on a bench that Johnny and I had made for just such a time as this. I rehearsed all the talks that we had sitting on this little bench. The temperature seemed cold to me as the sweat dried on my face, but in reality, it was 65 degrees—quite a contrast to 115 degrees inside the building.

Once lunch was behind me, I evaluated the process. The gold was not yet fully liquefied, but it was evident that the process was underway as the crud started floating to the top of the gold. I put on the thick gloves that reached all the way to my elbows. It was quite a challenge to hold the carbon rods that were necessary to remove the impurities from the gold. This is easier to do with a pair of vice grips, as I'd learned from experience. All the impurities attach themselves to the carbon rod, and I used one rod after another for the next two hours through stage one in the purification process.

As I worked, my mind went back to the story Johnny told the first time I witnessed the purification of gold. He said, "You know, Chuck, that carbon rod represents Jesus Christ. He became flesh that He may remove our sins and give us hope to reach our potential. And He lives forevermore to guard us against impurities from creeping back into our lives." He ended the story that day quoting 1 John 1:9, "If we confess our sins, He is faithful and just to forgive us our sins, and to cleanse us from all unrighteousness."

Afterward came the most dangerous time in the purification process, the pouring of the gold into sand molds. My focus must be complete during this, lest I put myself in danger. I put a vice grip on each side of the graphite pot to serve as handles as I poured. Gold, you see, will not stick to sand. It will leave a rough impression, but the sand will not attach itself to the pure gold that it cradled.

Once that was finished, I put the cauldron back, filled it with gold nuggets, and the process began all over again. As the gold hardens in the molds, I retrieve it, place it back in the Borax detergent and watch as the sand releases from the gold. There are always a few small bits of sand that refuse to let go. There are two ways to deal with this problem. The gold must either be pressure-washed or beaten loose with a hammer. Both represent the trying of our faith. We have the opportunity to wash ourselves in the water of the Word or the trials of this life will jar us loose from the things that try to hold us.

I found my rhythm. By the time the first batch was done, another was ready to be poured. The whole process may take me into the night, but it takes too long to get everything ready again. So I could not stop until all the gold had been purified. The heat, as well as the work, wore me down but the reward for my labor encouraged me as the nuggets increased in value. When the smelting pot held the last few nuggets I smiled. I'd be able to finish in the next few hours, maybe around 7:00 or so.

The time finally came to pour the last batch into the sand molds and shut down the ovens. You don't just flip a switch on this one, for even after the oxygen and fuel are cut off, the high temperatures are still dangerous for the hours that follow. I'd return to double check on everything before I went to bed. And besides all that, the ultimate clean-up couldn't be done for days. That saved time. I wanted to make sure everything was safe.

I had to admit, I was glad to see the day come to an end, but it had to be done. I felt as though I've been through a purifying myself as I locked the door, set the alarm, and made my way across the yard.

I shed my clothes in the utility room, placing them in the washing machine, even starting the machine before I showered. It seemed as though I sweat a gallon of water and I drank maybe two! I placed an order for pizza before getting in the shower. I was about out of steam myself.

I made it out of the shower ahead of the pizza guy, but the load in the washer was not yet done. Who knows, I thought, I may have just enough time to fix me a big glass of tea and enjoy my recliner for a few minutes.

Thumbing through the Bible, I stopped at 1 Peter chapter 1 and I began to read. The Holy Spirit struck a chord in my heart at verses six and seven, "Wherein ye greatly rejoice, though now for a season, if need be, ye are in heaviness through manifold temptation: That the trial of your faith, being much more precious than of gold that perisheth, though it be tried with fire, might be found unto praise and honour and glory at the appearing of Jesus Christ."

Suddenly I heard a knock at the door, and had to leave it right there for the moment. Yep, it was the pizza delivery guy bringing supper. I tipped him well and sent him on his way. The pizza was piping hot so I set it on the table, taking advantage of a moment to fill out my journal while it cools down. It seems appropriate, for the entire day had been hurry up and wait. Why should it stop with supper?

I wrote the title for today's entry: Purification by Fire. What have I learned?

- Fire can destroy or it can purify.
- God is a consuming fire.
- Difficult times build strong people.
- God is always there even in the midst of hardship.
- God desires to make you better and not bitter.
- The bigger the test, the bigger the testimony.
- We're all still in the process of purification.

With a second entry complete, I turned to my pizza and then to my bed to sleep on all I'd encountered. All in all, I must admit that it had been a great day. "I want to thank you, Lord, for always being with me. I know for certain that you are with me right now and you have promised to never leave me!" I prayed.

In this prayer, I find rest. I know I must always let tomorrow care of itself. Not ready to face it tonight; I'll need the hope that the sunrise will bring! The Bible instructs us all in Matthew 6:34, "Take therefore no thought for the morrow: for the morrow shall take thought for the things of itself…" And that sounds good to me. "Good night, Lord!"

Chapter 3

Shape Up Before You Ship Out

Sleeping in this morning felt pretty good. It was my first day off since I went back to work on Wednesday. I would have to set aside every Saturday to work on the project if I hoped to get it done on time. It got off to a great start, but today my time would be limited. With a quick look at my clock, I discovered that I hardly slept in at all—it's barely 6:30 AM. But the extra hour and a half still fared better than getting up at 5 o'clock every morning to make the trek to Carson City, a trip I can make with my eyes closed. I remember it like it was yesterday. When I was hired at the FedEx distribution center, the HR manager asked me if I was going to be moving from Fallon to Carson City. I still remember my reply as I simply said, "We'll see!"

I guess we've seen, since that was nearly twenty-four years ago and I still live in Fallon. I was born here and I guess I'll die here. I prefer living in a small town with 8,450 people I know to living in a big city with 54,830 plus that I don't know. You see, I'm a country boy at heart and I'm more than willing to commute more than two hours a day to stay right here.

From Fallon, you can be in Carson City or Reno within an hour if you need to go there. But the skyscrapers blocked my view of the Sierra Nevada Mountain range. And for that reason I will forever say, "No, thank you!" I have to stay close to these mountains. They hold so many memories for me as well as the history of our nation.

It's a little known fact that Nevada has richer deposits of silver and gold than anywhere in our nation. California gets all the publicity, but Nevada has the gold. Seventy-five percent of our nation's gold came from these Nevada Mountains. But I guess the abundance of silver found here caused the gold to be overshadowed in the record books. That's actually fine with me since it's left our region basically the same as it was over two hundred years ago. The truth of the matter is that we are much richer here in many places. We are red-blooded Americans who are true patriots at heart. We love our country, respect our flag, and root for our football team, the Reno Wolf Pack. We have the greatest football rivalry in our nation between the Wolf Pack of the University of Nevada Reno and the Running Rebels of UNLV, the University of Nevada Las Vegas.

Since 1970, we have been playing for the Fremont Cannon, the most expensive trophy in all of football, including the Super Bowl. Our Wolf Pack leads the series 25-15 and presently we are in an 8-year winning streak. Once again, UNLV gets most of our nation's attention, but you will find the trophy resting at Mackey Stadium in Reno. We hold the record as well as the bragging rights. That's what would limit my work on the project this day. I promised to take JD to the opening game between the Wolf Pack and the Running Rebels at 3:00 PM.

Mackey Stadium will be packed to the hilt and rocking with 30,000 screaming fans. We planned to be two of them! Boy, I wish Johnny could be with us, but he would certainly expect us to continue the tradition—and that we will.

I had better get going; I seemed to be moving slowly, and time was clicking away. While the coffee brewed, I read my devotion. Today's scripture is found in Proverbs 22:6, "Train up a child in the way he should go: and when he is old, he will not depart from it." This verse came across a little strange to me personally since I only have nieces and nephews. I read on.

The writer followed the scripture with an explanation of what it really means to raise up a child. This verse translates to raise him up in the way he is bent and not according to our own selfish desires. We should examine each child with his God-given gifts and proclivities and shape him to fulfill God's desired plan. We are not the same; in fact, none of us even carry the same fingerprint, much less the same destiny.

The signal on the coffee pot told me that my coffee was ready and my resting time over. I took my mug to the workshop; it often served as a welcome friend in the cool autumn weather.

I flipped on the lights and headed straight to the heater to knock the chill off the building. I hoped it would get a jump on warming things up as I ran to the truck to retrieve my package. One of the blessings of working at FedEx is that we are able to get our shipments more quickly than most people and they always arrive before the weekend. I stepped back in the shop and noticed right away things were warming up quite nicely. Time to get to work.

I picked up a screwdriver and ran it down the seam of tape on the first box. I'm greeted with thousands of little Styrofoam peanuts protecting the kit necessary for gold plating. In the other box is my blade. I thought I'd never get the right one since there are hundreds of shaped blades and I have had zero experience. The research alone had taken me hours at night to find. In fact, it took longer to find it than it did to get it here. I'm reminded of my devotion as I hold the blade in my hand. You've got to know your purpose before you start your process.

Once I researched commemorative swords, I settled on the traditional English court sword. It's used to commemorate special covenantal agreements. Traditionally it is made of pure silver, but our version would be a little different; it will be made of gold and silver to represent the people of this area. I doubt if you'd even be able to recognize it after we put our Nevada twist on it. The blade arrives blank, ready to be shaped based on my purpose and plan that I designed for it. I would have to be extremely careful in the process because there's no way I can add back to the sword what's been extracted from it. I knew this will be a painstaking process.

As I turn on my grinding wheel, a lump formed in my throat as I placed the blade against the guide with all the calibrations set. I've chosen to use the smoothest stone until I become more comfortable. I examined the plans over and over, calculating every dimension.

I sure wished Johnny was here! He was old hat at these things. He could do it with his eyes closed. That's not the case with me and it has to be right. I've got only one chance in shaping it correctly and it's really important, more important, in fact, than I realize.

I'm coming to believe that shaping young lives is even more important and Johnny had become a pro at this as well. For over twenty years, he had served as Scout Master for our local Boy Scout troop here in Fallon. He also had served on the Board of Directors of the Boy Scouts for the state of Nevada. It's hard to say just how many lives he shaped to help them fulfill their destinies, or how many current leaders in our state operate in their daily lives based on what he has taught them about honesty and service. He knew how to exert the right pressure at the right time in the right place to help them be shaped individually to fulfill the personal plan for their life. As I think about that, I'm glad my project is just a hunk of silver. At least if I miss the mark, I can buy another blank. But believe me, I don't want to do it. This thing was very expensive.

I find myself doing a lot more measuring than grinding and buffing, but things are beginning to take shape. As often is the case, it's hard to tell when you're making progress. But eventually, I was almost there. The clock on the wall read 11:00 AM and to be honest, I was a nervous wreck; this is tedious work. Part of the struggle in shaping metal is that you must keep everything clean while you are shaping since the oil of your hands can leave residue on the blades that will affect the plating process. I'd already changed my cotton gloves twice to ensure I left the blade undefiled.

The same principle is true in shaping lives. We don't need to leave our fingerprints on the people, since we are nothing more than an extension of the hands of Christ. Only He should be seen and we should be hidden behind the work of the cross. This is so difficult since we ourselves have experienced so many faults and failures. We tend to try to shape the blade to cover our mistakes rather than God's intended plan.

My calibrations finally indicated that I arrived. Everything looked good to the naked eye, but even more importantly, it matched the dimensions of the plan. It was still just a chunk of metal, but it would for sure be a sword one day. The die had been cast and the plans laid; I must now commit myself to what I have started. I have just enough time to read the instructions for the next steps in the gold plating process. But that will have to wait until next Saturday.

You see, there are six steps in the process:

Invest in everything you are going to need to accomplish the task. That reminds me of the words of Jesus, "Before a man builds a house, let him count the cost." Everything that pays dividends in our lives must first begin with an investment. So many people want to reap where they have not sown. We must first be willing to pay the price. I guess I can put a checkmark beside that one.

Consider what you are willing to gold plate. All metals are not the same, and not all metals are worth the investment of gold for the labor that it will take to complete it. Boy, that's certainly true. You sure don't want to gold plate a tin can. Make sure you're investing in someone who is worth your investment and time. When you do it right, it will only increase their value.

Make sure the item is kept completely clean and pure in the entire bonding process. I'm so thankful that I knew this much anyway before I got started. This required:

Wear cloth gloves—check!

Use solutions and buff with new buffing wheel—check!

Wipe clean to remove all residue—check!

Place item in distilled water. If the water glides smoothly from the item without beading and forming droplets, then the item is clean—check!

Dry the item again with a clean cloth to make it ready for the next step in the bonding process—check!

Wrap the item in a linen cloth and place it back in the box—check!

The other two have to do with the next step so I used the rest of my time to let off some steam and unwind. My plan was for us to grab a bite to eat before we head to the big game. To try to eat at Mackey Stadium is like trying to eat a bowl of chili while riding a horse and jumping fences; it's nearly impossible. Anyway, I was ready for a good meal in a quiet place.

After yet another shower, I jump into the truck and head toward Johnny's house. I'm going to have to stop calling it that, but that may take some time. To be perfectly honest, I dreaded going over there, but all of us have to face things we don't want to do if we are going to minister to others in need. I've talked to Shirley and JD several times, but this will be the first time I've been there since I've heard of his death.

As I pulled in the yard, I noticed everything looked exactly the same, yet I knew everything has been made completely different with the absence of just one person. Shirley meets me at the door and says, "Hey Chuck, how are you doing?"

I smile as I hug her and replied, "I'm OK—how are you?"

She smiled through her pain. "I guess I'm adjusting; I have to. JD still needs me to be there for him." We both nodded in agreement as tears filled our eyes.

About the same time, JD bounded down the steps. With a huge grin on his face, he blurted out, "Hey Uncle Chuck, how are you doing?"

"I'm fine. How are you, my man?"

He gave me a high five. "I am ready for this game. This is going to be awesome, dude, to watch the Wolf Pack stomp a hole in the Running Rebels and to send them running back, crying all the way to Las Vegas. Well, are you ready to go?" he asked.

"You bet!"

With a hug from Shirley for both of us, we headed toward the truck to make our way to the game.

"JD, where do you want to eat?" I was hoping he would choose some nice, quiet, out of the way place, but I forgot that he was a twelve-year-old kid.

"How about Dairy Queen? All the kids hang out there."

"That place would be louder than Mackey Stadium," I thought to myself. I had to remind myself once again that this is not about me, it's about him. This day belongs to JD.

We made it through our Dairy Queen meal, though it was anything but relaxing. We climbed back in the truck and headed toward Reno. I glanced frequently at JD as we rode along over the next hour. My mind was filled with hundreds of questions, but I strongly felt that I should allow him to steer the conversation. Most of the talk was centered on the game and how badly we were going to rub their face in the grass under the Fremont Cannon.

He only mentioned Johnny one time during the conversation and it was in relation to the homework that he had to make up while he was out for the funeral. He had returned to school on Wednesday. I wanted to pry deeper but all I could think about was that metal blade and how shaping it was such a tedious process; the right pressure at the right place at the right time. It was abundantly clear that it was not the time. The last thing he needed was to feel responsible for ministering to me in my hurts; he was just a kid and he had gone through enough role reversals. He needed me to be a positive role model who would put his feelings above my own. Now was a time to build trust and to have fun. That is exactly what we were going to do.

As we drove into the parking lot, it was obvious that the stadium was filled to capacity, just as we had pictured. We had to push our way through the crowd at the stadium to find our season seats. We had no sooner sat down when he looked over at me and said, "You think we ought to get some nachos and a Coke before the game gets started?" I realized I just received my marching orders. I thought to myself, "We just ate an hour ago." But I had forgotten how much it takes to fill up a twelve-year-old boy! I made my way to the concession stand and got everything on the list; we were set to watch the game. Boy, was it a doozy!

The Wolf Pack was furious right out of the gate, as they set their plan in motion to tear the Rebels apart. The pistol formation fired on every cylinder and we took an early lead. Somewhere in the middle of the first half, he looked over at me and said, "Uncle Chuck, do you think Papaw is watching this?" I fought to hold back my emotions, stuck up my thumb and said, "You bet he is—

he wouldn't dare miss this one!" The answer seemed to satisfy him as he turned his attention back toward the field. We hooped and hollered till we nearly lost our voices rooting the Wolf Pack to a 28-14 victory. We had doubled their score and it was a great day.

We made our way back to the truck and headed home. He fell asleep almost immediately as he leaned against the door. I was again left with my thoughts as I wondered if I had passed the test and had done everything right. I felt a lot more nervous than I did with the silver blade this morning that was for sure! I finally came to the conclusion that just like the metal blade, all I could do was deal with what had surfaced and wait for the next step in the journey. The thought kept coming to my mind, Handle with Care, and it seemed to bring peace to my heart.

As we pulled up in the yard, he woke up as Shirley flipped on the porch light. I said, "We're home, my man!"

He unbuckled his seat belt and jumped from the truck to the ground.

Before he closed the door, he peeped inside and said, "Thanks a lot, Uncle Chuck. This was the greatest day of my life." He ran up the driveway toward Shirley as she waved from the porch. I gave a honk on the horn as I backed out of the driveway and began to make my way toward home.

His statement kept haunting me: This is the greatest day of my life. How in the world could he say that after his Papaw had tragically died in a fire just one week ago? The answer was simple. He had learned to live in the moment while I was still stuck in the past. Then the thought hit my mind, Who's helping who? Maybe it's me that needs to learn from him how to get over the past and embrace the moment. One thing was certain, we had just made our first memory for the future together. When all is said and done, that's life. What we have learned and the memories we keep.

As I pulled in my driveway, I turned off my truck and looked where the mountains touch the sky. I realize that there is a new day that will dawn that is now hidden in darkness on the other side of the mountain. I said to the Lord, "Thank you for the greatest day of my life today. Help me to live one day at a time."

I walked into my house and there on the table were my devotional, my Bible, and my journal. These three books had become my new three-fold cord that could not be broken. As I read my Bible, one scripture kept coming to my mind so I turned to Jeremiah 29:11 in the New International Version. It reads, "For I know the plans I have for you, declares the Lord, plans to prosper you and not to harm you, plans to give you hope and a future."

I laid down my Bible and picked up my journal. What should I call my entry for today? Shape Up Before You Ship Out. What lessons have I learned?

- God has a plan for my life.
- He's shaping me every day to fulfill His plan.
- Shaping is a process of grinding and buffing.
- God knows exactly what He is doing.
- There's always grace to handle what surfaces.
- Live for today; embrace the moment.
- Put tomorrow in God's hands.

I'm sure there are many more lessons to be learned but I've had about all I can handle for today. It was time to hit the hay and rest up for the next trek in this great adventure.

Chapter 4

Strength for His Purpose

A thick frost greeted me as I pulled back the curtains to view the day; sunlight glistens off the trees as the sun peers over the mountain driving the shadows toward the valley below as another Saturday morning announces its arrival. No doubt, fall is here and winter is soon approaching. Most people view Nevada as a desert because of Las Vegas and Death Valley which are so well known, yet up in the northern mountain region the weather can be quite different, especially when the arctic blast mixes with the high altitude. We certainly have all four seasons here.

Nothing on the agenda today would hinder me from returning to the project. The Wolfpack is on the road, and JD is on a scouting retreat, so I feel as if I'm on my own. It has been three weeks since I've had opportunity do any work but I'm sure everything would be lying right where I left it. Mowing the leaves at Shirley's and around this place as well, winterizing our houses and cars, these preparations had kept me busy. Things that had to be done and someone had to do them. They had fallen to my lot. But I really didn't mind at all.

Breakfast out sounded good this morning. I usually eat light through the week since I have to get up so early but today I wanted to begin things with my belly full. But first, I needed to enjoy my coffee and feed my spirit man. I established a good routine over these last days, and I don't want to interrupt that, although life does sometimes throw us curve balls and our schedules get out of control. In times like that, we just have to do the best we can. Yet

I don't feel pushed this particular morning, so I'm not going to change my routine.

With coffee in one hand and the devotional in the other, I head toward my recliner sensing an unusual peace that I have not quite figured out. Maybe it's because of the anticipation of the word God has in store for me.

I thumb through my devotional until I come across my reading. It's simply entitled Strength for His Purpose. The story is about a man named Paul Anderson who held the title for years in the late sixties as the "World's Strongest Man." His story was quite touching; as a young boy he lost his parents and was placed in an orphan's home. He was the runt in the family and quickly became the punching bag around the orphanage. Every kid's frustrations were taken out on him. Little Paul had no one to defend his cause. The constant abuse gave him every right to become bitter, but he chose instead to release his frustration to God as he became a man of prayer. He took constant inventory of his life as he continued to grow and he decided that he would maximize what he had instead of whining over what he had lost.

In the process he adopted this motto for life: "In my weakness, His strength is made perfect." Though he was short in stature, he became stronger than other kids, even those who were twice his size. Consequently, he pursued body building, all the while looking for ways to use what he had for God's glory while seeking His direction. His prayer was simple: "Lord, you created me for your purpose. Now use me for your glory."

As his strength began to increase, the bullying certainly declined. Yet Paul chose not to retaliate. He realized that their abuse was nothing more than a demonstration of their own pain and he knew exactly how they felt. He too had been kicked from pillar to post. His body-building continued with amazing results as he found himself climbing through the ranks with trophies stacking up along the way. From local competitions to regional to state to national and international, each step graced with the favor of God and the recognition of people, as God began to unfold His purpose in Paul's life.

One day, just before the World Championships Paul had an encounter with God. Praying offstage, he made the promise that if God would allow him to become the world's strongest man, he would use his platform and wealth to open orphanages and help other kids for the rest of his life. God did and so did Paul. He's helped hundreds of orphaned children to turn their tragedy to triumph. Man, I loved this story! Especially the title: Strength for His Purpose.

What a great thought as I picked up my keys and wallet and headed for the door. When I opened the storm door, the cold wind slapped me in the face like an angry foe. How cold is it anyway? I wondered. The thermometer hanging on my garage read 28 degrees. Wow! This was the coldest day of the year so far. It's that time of year that the temperature can vary by forty to fifty degrees in a single day. You don't really know what to wear or what you will face. In fact, we all say around these parts, "If you don't like the weather, stick around, it's subject to change."

The wind had the leaves swirling around me as I jumped into the truck. I pause for just a moment to take in all the colors. A beautiful thought came to my mind—Even in death, there is beauty for those that have eyes to see! These beautiful colors were brought about by harsh temperatures and winds of adversity that had changed the landscape over time. Yet what the untrained eye cannot see is that the sap is going back to the roots to prepare for new growth for spring. These leaves are a victim of a change of seasons. It's just a cycle of life. Life has a mixture of both good and bad. If we don't lose hope, there's a springtime awaiting us as well.

I thought I could actually hear the ham and eggs calling my name across town. This prompted me to get a move on. As I pulled across the parking lot of Jerry's Restaurant, I saw that I was not the only one with Saturday morning eating plans. This place was packed! I made my way through the door where inside everyone greets me, some verbally while others just threw up their hand. I am warmed by that gratifying feeling that I am among friends.

I took a seat at the counter since I don't like sitting in a booth by myself. About that time, Jenny walked up.

"Hi Chuck! What are you drinking today?" she asked cheerfully.

I answered, "My normal—coffee and water."

"Do you know what you want to eat?" she inquired.

"Sure do, ma'am. Ham and eggs over medium. And add a piping hot short stack."

"Somebody's eating high on the hog this morning." She smiled as she made her way to the kitchen. I picked up the newspaper and begin to read the headlines. As she returns with my coffee and water she asks, "Chuck, how's Shirley and JD doing?"

I paused before answering. "They seem to be fine for what they are facing. JD's on a retreat this weekend with the Boy Scouts."

"Yeah, my boy, Billy's on the same retreat," she interrupted. "They are pretty good friends, you know. I think the retreat was a great idea to give the boys the opportunity to connect with a new scout master. It will give them a chance to work through their feelings as well. There's a lot of little boys out there that looked to Johnny Dale as a father figure. I certainly know that Billy did. He has sure struggled since Rob was killed."

She paused for a moment, looked me in the eyes, and said confidently, "Maybe you should get involved in the program. It might do you some good."

"I don't know about that one, Jenny. I'm not sure I'm the fathering kind."

She smiled and assured me, "I'll bet you would be a dandy! I'd better leave that idea right here and get to scooting. This place is hopping this morning."

It sure seemed to be taking a while to get my food this morning, but that can be expected with such a crowd. Unfortunately, there wasn't a lot of news either. Right on cue, Jenny showed up with my food and an apology about it taking so long. I assured her that it was fine, I was in no big hurry. Yet I tore right into it like I hadn't eaten in a week. Man, it hit the spot.

Once again, I was reminded of how many lives Johnny's life

had touched. I also found companionship in the pain of others as we all struggled to deal with our loss. Then my thoughts went to Jenny and how difficult it must be as a single mom raising a son on a waitress' salary while trying to fill both spots as a father and a mother to a young boy. The very thought gripped my heart. I slipped twenty dollars under the plate as a tip and headed to pay my bill. As I was standing in line, she passed by, gently patted me on the shoulder and said, "Thanks, Chuck."

I said, "No problem. See you later." She smiled over her shoulder as she disappeared through the kitchen door. I, on the other hand, hopped in my truck and headed toward home. Pulling into the yard, I went straight for the work shed. I was afraid of what might happen if those ham and eggs collided with the recliner; I may not wake up until dark!

As I opened the door and hit the light switch, everything was just as I had left it, as if it were waiting patiently on me to find time for the next stage in the process. I retrieved the silver blade from the box. I call it silver though in reality, there's about a ten percent copper mix in the blade to add strength, since silver and gold are both too soft a metal to use as a blade. They will bend under the pressure.

Copper is also one of our rich deposits here in Nevada. One of the largest deposits ever found is in Yerington, only an hour from here. It was the first copper mine opened in this state in 1865. Gold, silver, and copper represent the strength of the people found around here. They are pure and strong.

As I unwrap the blade, the light reflects down the metal like lightning. It is spotless, but next it must be stressed before I can plate it. That can only happen through tempering. There is no new way to temper metal; it must be done the same way as it has traditionally been done for hundreds of years. Unless you are a trained silversmith or blacksmith, you can do more harm than good in the tempering process. In this process, the temperature must be balanced and regulated and the cooling must be done with precise timing. This is where wisdom trumps ambition and ego and is another valuable lesson that Johnny taught me. "Don't overthink the process!" he would say. He simply used a conventional oven to temper silver since the metal only has to be heated to 550 degrees to accomplish the task.

Having learned from him, I merely reach over and turn on the oven to 550 degrees and waited for it to preheat. This day's work would not be labor intensive but mostly about timing and patience. Johnny built us a firebrick slab to fit just inside the oven. Crudely made of a long metal tray lined with firebrick to retain and distribute the heat, while the metal tray beneath serves as a flat surface to prevent the blade from warping. It did the job.

In no time at all, the oven beeps and it was time to begin the process. I placed the blade on the brick and gently slid it through the oven door. The heat would do the work but that does not mean I can leave the blade unattended. After all, I'm not baking a cake, I'm tempering metal, and that process requires that I watch the color chart for the heating of the metal. It runs from a dull red at 500 degrees to a pure white at 1300 and above. My perimeters today are to keep it between dull red and deep red. The ideal temperature is 550 degrees. With the oven, there is a built in safeguard keeping me from destroying the very blade I'm trying to develop. I feel in control somehow today, even though the oven is doing the work. It gave me the opportunity to multitask.

One part of the sword I needed to work on next is the hilt. The hilt is a small piece that goes between the blade and the handle. Its purpose is two-fold: One is to set the boundary as to how far the blade can penetrate; the second is to protect the one using the sword. I chose to make it a polished silver since the handle guard will be made of gold.

I began the work of cutting out the pattern designed from the small piece of silver that I'd ordered for the job. It always amazes me to look at a blank piece of metal with an understanding of what it will become hidden only in my mind. It makes me think of the words of Michelangelo when he was asked about his statue of David and how he approached the marble slab. He said, "My job is to remove all the marble that is not David." That's kind of true. All creative minds remove what is standing between them and their masterpiece.

With earplugs in and goggles on, I divide my time between cutting, grinding, polishing, and watching. It takes around 2 hours and 15 minutes to reach the desirable color in the blade and about 1 hour and 45 minutes more to cool down. I'll have to repeat this process three times, so it looks like another full day ahead.

When the clock pushed twelve o'clock, I noticed that my ham and eggs were nothing more than a memory. Lunch was in order before I repeated the heating cycle. As I walk to the house I noticed that all of the frost had vanished and the sun was shining brightly. It's a beautiful day in Fallon; the temperature has more than doubled and it's a lot more comfortable than it was this morning. Humans are comfort creatures, you know. More interested in comfort than progress.

Returning from lunch, I could see that the preheat oven light had kicked back on and the next session was ready to begin. Time for me to get back to the hilt as the blade goes through the next step in the tempering process. It looks like my plan to multitask is coming off without a hitch. I love it when a plan comes together!

As I work, I decided to slightly curve the ends of the hilt so that it will blend more with the hand guard, which will be gold plated as well. This should be a nice added touch. You have to be extremely careful in heating polished silver that contains copper lest you cause it to yellow. I will once again have to use slow heat to make my bends in the metal. It may take a couple of hours to do it but it will be worth it for the added contour effect.

The second session ends on time—four o'clock or so. I start the oven for the third and final round as I button up the final touches on the hilt. Everything looked perfect and all that's left is to polish the hilt and wait for the blade to heat to a perfect color.

As I admired my day's work, I couldn't help but think of the watchful eye of God over His children. He has promised that He will never leave us, nor forsake us, yet that does not mean that we won't go through the furnace. But we can rest in His wisdom and find comfort in knowing that the gentle touch of His skillful hand is shaping us just right in the place that He has designed for us.

At 6:45 I cut off the oven for the final time. The cooling stage is underway; the blade will be safe right where it is. I've got the hilt polished and put away. Everything is ready for the next step. I must admit that I feel a real sense of pride and accomplishment as I lock the shed and head toward the house. Its growing dark, but I know the sun will rise again in a few hours and the process will start all over again.

A can of soup is on the menu for supper and while it heats, I write a few notes in my journal. I'm beginning to understand better what James meant when he said in James 1:2-4, "My brethren, count it all joy when ye fall into divers temptations; Knowing this, that the trying of your faith worketh patience. But let patience have her perfect work, that ye may be perfect and entire, wanting nothing."

I title this day's entry Strength for His Purpose, the same as my morning devotion. What have I learned?

- God is always with us, even in the trials.
- The heat is meant to temper us, not destroy us.
- He sets every boundary to protect us.
- Tempering strengthens us for warfare.
- We are all under the watchful eye of God.
- God will not allow us to be tempted past our strength to stand.
- It's all about His ultimate purpose and plan.

My bubbling soup called me to supper. I had plenty of time to relax for a little while and then get ready for church tomorrow. Though really it seems like lately I am more aware of His presence every moment. Thank you Lord for being my constant companion!

Chapter 5

Iron Sharpens Iron

My perfect night's sleep was interrupted by an unannounced battle between my eyes and the early morning sun. Apparently, my curtains are perfectly poised to expose my entire pillow to the morning and there was no retreat in sight! I shifted around a time or two until I was ready to surrender to my foe.

As I sat up on the side of the bed, I saw the time. It was eight o'clock! Maybe I've won the battle after all; this is the latest I have slept in a month. I needed to get a move on, however, for today is going to be a doozy!

I have an appointment with a silversmith at ten o'clock. I reached the place in my process where I needed to solicit help from a professional. There are just some things that you cannot do alone. Once again, I'm reminded that we all have limits. I suppose God has created us that way to open the door to new relationships in our lives. It's great to know our strengths, but maybe even greater to know our weaknesses. Once we come to grips with them, progress is imminent.

Today is also a great day for football. The Wolf Pack is in town and will be playing at Mackey Field at three o'clock. I've asked Jenny and Billy to join JD and me to watch the big game against the Boise State Broncos, the second biggest rival in our division. The Wolf Pack is having a stellar season this year; we're 12-1. Our only loss was against the Honolulu Warriors when they played them on October 16. We probably wouldn't have lost that one if JD and I had been there to cheer them on to victory!

A win both today and next Saturday would clinch our opportunity for a bowl game, something a little unusual in our division. The Kraft Hunger Bowl will be held at AT&T Park in San Francisco on January 9th. But I guess we shouldn't count our chickens before they hatch and we certainly don't want to look past Boise State. These guys are tough and they always ramp up to play the Wolf Pack. Today should shape up to be a real battle. It is our homecoming and the last home game of the year.

I grabbed my coffee, sat at the table, picked up my devotional, and turned to November 27. The devotion was another true story about a man named Nicky Cruz.

Nicky was raised in the slums of New York City. He lost his father when was just a kid and found himself growing up on the streets of the Big Apple. Life was not easy for Nicky; he had to learn to fight to survive and fighting had become a way of life. What he lacked in size, he made up for in spirit. He joined the gangs at an early age, drawn by his need for family. He quickly ascended in the ranks. There was nothing that Nicky wouldn't do and no one that he was afraid to confront.

His whole life centered on drugs, prostitution, crime, and murder; he ultimately became the most feared man in his neighborhood. Then one day, a skinny, naïve preacher from Pennsylvania showed up on Nicky's turf with nothing but a call of God on his life. His lack of money forced him to sleep in his car, not exactly the safest thing to do. He was awakened by the sound of his hubcaps being stolen. As he looked out the window, he saw a bunch of kids practicing for the gang life awaiting them. He got his hubcaps back but got much more than he could ever expect as Nicky and his gang made their way down the street toward him.

The young preacher, David Wilkerson, thought that this would be the perfect group with which to share the Gospel. It did not go as planned. The preacher began to share and Nicky stopped him dead in his tracks and told him that he didn't want to hear it. Things seriously escalated when David asked Nicky, "What are you afraid of? I only want to tell you about the love of Jesus Christ."

Nicky pulled out his switchblade, slung it open, grabbing the preacher by the arm, and said, "I'm not afraid of anything! I'll take this knife and cut you up into a thousand pieces."

He must have thought, "This will shut the mouth of this country preacher." But David Wilkerson could not be threatened. He looked Nicky straight in the eye and replied, "And all one thousand pieces will tell you that Jesus loves you!"

The story goes on to tell the conversion and the call of Nicky Cruz to the ministry of Jesus Christ. Wow! Such boldness can only be driven by a love that is greater than fear, a love great enough to confront.

Finishing off my last sip of coffee, I set the cup in the sink, filled it with water, picked up my keys, and headed for the door. If I use my time wisely, I might just be able to grab a bite to eat before my appointment. So I headed across town to Jerry's. I took a seat at the counter as everyone nodded and waved. Jenny gathered the silverware, water, and menu and headed my way.

"Good morning, Chuck," she said with a smile. "How was your Thanksgiving?"

"OK, I guess. It certainly wasn't my best one, that's for sure. How was yours?"

"It was good; really good! Boy, we are looking forward to the game this afternoon. I sure appreciate you inviting me and Billy to come along."

"You're more than welcome. It'll be a real treat for the boys. I must admit, I'm looking forward to it myself. I need to get my mind on something else for a little while."

"Me, too!" she said. "I just can't believe I'm off on a Saturday afternoon. That doesn't happen to me much around here. What can I get you to eat this morning?"

"I believe I will have an egg sandwich and a cup of coffee."

"Wow, you're eating light this morning!" she said, looking up from the pad.

"Yeah, but I plan to make up for it later!"

As she retreated to the kitchen, I couldn't stop thinking about the story I had read and how much courage it must have taken for David Wilkerson to stand up to a street gang. Only love could make a man do that. His love for God and his love for others would have to exceed his own life. No man on earth could resist that kind of love.

I was lost in my thoughts when Jenny returned with my breakfast. She sat the plate on the table, filled my coffee cup, and walked away, leaving me in my silence. I said grace and began to eat my sandwich, while putting myself in that situation.

I began to think about what it would have been like to have been every character in the scene. Jenny came by with the coffee pot to warm up my coffee and she said, "A penny for your thoughts this morning."

"I'll have to tell you later because it's more like a dollar's worth," I replied.

"OK," she said. "What time will you be by?"

"Between 1:00 and 1:15. That should give us enough time."

"Alright. I'll be ready. See you then." She left my ticket on the counter and she walked away. I paid the ticket, left a tip, and headed toward the door.

As I started the truck, I began to fumble through my pockets looking for the address to Peggy's Pretty Pieces. What a strange place to find a blacksmith! The "Open" sign in the front window greeted me as I made my way up three small steps. I triggered the bell as I opened the door; it rang out clearly announcing my arrival. This place was full of trinkets and dainty knick-knacks. It certainly wasn't the stable I expected but a deep voice broke the silence from the back of the building.

"Hello. Can I help you?"

I responded, "Yes, hello! I'm Chuck Haynes. I have a ten o'clock appointment."

From behind the wall stepped a huge man in his early sixties, dressed like a cowboy with a waxed handlebar mustache adorning his wrinkled face. His hand swallowed mine as he announced himself, "I'm Max Hammons. Good to meet you, Chuck. You're the one that wants me to sharpen the sword blade?"

"Yep, that's me," I said. I set the blade on the counter and began to unwrap it.

"Wow! That's a pretty thing," Max said. "What kind of sword is that, anyway?"

"It's an English court sword, used to commemorate special occasions. I have a lot of plans for this blade but I want to put an edge on it before I do anything else."

"Yep, I understand," he agreed. "Do you want an edge on both sides of the blade or just one?"

"I think a two-edged sword would be great but I plan to do some engraving on it later. Do you think I will have enough room?"

"I think so," Max said. "A double-edged blade would really set this thing off."

I see this as an opening to share my faith with Max. So I blurted out, "A two-edged sword reminds me of the Bible."

"OK," he replied. "I'd better get started."

"Do you mind if I watch you do it?" I asked.

"I don't usually allow a lot of people in the shop area. But I guess it won't hurt anything. Come on back."

His blacksmith shop looked a lot more of what I had in mind; a huge contrast between it and the gift shop up front. But it was obvious that a lot of the trinkets had been birthed out of the ashes back here.

On the workbench was a grinder like nothing I had ever seen before. I took a seat on a huge wire spool sitting just to the left. It looked like the perfect seat to view this process. Max began measuring, figuring, and writing down everything on a yellow legal pad as if I were not present at all. The silence grew awkward but I didn't want to break his concentration.

Finally, he took the blade, fastened it to the guide and locked it in place. He began to type in all the dimensions on a computer system. Reaching under the bench, he pulled out a pair of goggles. He said, "You may want to put these on. There's going to be a lot of sparks flying around here in a minute when this grinding wheel goes to work on your pretty blade."

Flipping the switch, he went to work, sharpening the blade with expert precision. The war was on and the grinding wheel was winning, but the whole process was being guided by the hands of a master. That was evident. This blade would never be the same.

I watched in amazement as he completed the first side of the blade. Flipping off the grinder, he looked it over and placed the blade back in the guide for the other side. I sat there wondering if I should ask him if he were a Christian. To me, he looked scarier than Nicky Cruz! He was a man's man and he hadn't actually responded too well to my Bible statement earlier. The more I thought about it, the more I convinced myself that if a Pennsylvania preacher could confront a New York gang leader, surely I could ask a cowboy!

"Hey, Max, are you a Christian?" There was a long pause following my question.

And then Max responded, "I certainly believe in the good Lord, if that's what you're asking. But to my understanding, the word Christian means to be like Christ. And I'm still working on that one! It's like sharpening this blade—He's been grinding on me for decades!"

The conversation ended as he started up the grinder for the other side of the blade. In a matter of minutes, he was finished. Then he turned on his polishing wheel and buffed out every mark the grinder had made. Once again, the blade looked brand new but this time it looked even better. Now it had a cutting edge both ways.

He made his way toward the front and I followed like a little pup. I squared up my bill, picked up my blade, and stuck out my right hand. "It was great to meet you, Max. I would love to invite you to come out to Christian Life Center some time. I think you would feel right at home."

He smiled and said, "Bring that thing back when you are finished. I'd love to see the whole thing put together." I promised him that I would as I made my way toward home.

I put everything away and headed toward the house to get ready for the game.

The first stop was Shirley's house to pick up JD. They were both in the yard as I pulled into the driveway. I could tell from the road that JD was ready for the ballgame as he made a beeline for the truck. Shirley waved as she made her way toward the house. JD hopped in and I pointed the truck toward Jenny's house.

I must admit; it was then that my nerves kicked in. It had been over twenty years since I've been on any kind of date—if you could call this a date! I kept assuring myself that it was more about the boys than it was about Jenny and me.

As we pulled up to Jenny's, JD reached over to honk the horn. I grabbed his hand and he said, "Give the horn a honk, Uncle Chuck, and let them know we are here!"

"I don't think so," I said. "You sit right here and I'll go get them."

Billy said, "Hi," as he headed for the truck to see JD. Jenny and I followed along behind. I opened the door to help her in the truck. I realized then that it wasn't exactly built for a lady.

The boys were in the back of the club cab and Jenny and I were sat up front. They were carried away, talking a mile a minute, but things were a little bit quieter in the front seat. Though conversation was never a problem at Jerry's Restaurant, it was a little different when she was sitting beside me in the truck. I think she could tell I was feeling a little awkward, so she broke the ice as she said, "You told me it would take some time to tell me your dollar story. We have an hour—what was on your mind this morning?"

I told her about my devotion today and how it challenged me to examine my own commitment to Christ and sharing the Gospel, something I've been struggling with since Thanksgiving.

"Thanksgiving?" she asked me.

I told her I wanted to spend it with Shirley and JD. But she felt it would be better for her and JD to start a new family tradition together. So I ended up spending Wednesday, Thursday, and Friday with my family. My brother and sister and their families came in for a few days.

"It wasn't that bad, was it?" she asked.

"No, I don't mean it that way. They're just always on my back about moving on with my life. I really don't have a lot of family. Mom and Dad were killed in a car wreck fifteen years ago. They were hit by a drunk driver, leaving me, my baby sister, Rachel, and older brother, Landon."

"Tell me about them. I'd love to know more."

"Well, Rachel is married to John Wallace. She met him in college. He's a lawyer for the state of California so they live in Sacramento. They have a ten-year-old boy named Ethan and a thirteen-year-old girl named Ellen. Landon is married to Renee and they pastor the Assembly of God Church in Ely, Nevada. They have two boys, Russell and Robert, but they are both grown. We all meet at my house every holiday, partly because Fallon is the halfway point for both of them and partly because it is still home to all of us since we were raised here. Enough about me; what about you and your family?"

"Rob and I both were from Houston, Texas. Actually Rob would interrupt me right here and say that he was from Galveston. But every suburb is Houston to me. We met at Rice University in our senior year. Rob came from a military family and he joined the Navy once he graduated. He had only one desire—to be a navy pilot. Therefore, after we were married, he was transferred here to the Fallon Navy base. Shortly thereafter, he was sent to Afghanistan and I stayed behind with Billy in Fallon. Rob was shot down January 9, 2005, just three months before he was supposed to return home."

"I'm sorry, Jenny, for interrupting. That must have been horrible!"

"Yes, it was," she continued. "But he died with honor doing what he loved to do. Life has its struggles but it's in the battles that the victories are won." The minutes clicked by as the conversation deepened.

"Well, guys, we're almost here. We need to get our game faces on and get this Wolf Pack growling!"

The game was amazing! The Wolf Pack pulled it out in overtime, 34-31. It was the sweetest victory after the most intense battle. It was an emotional roller coaster for all of us as we made our way back to the truck and started toward Fallon. The boys were elated because of the win and they were also jacked up on plenty of candy.

Jenny and I continued our conversation on the way home about tragedy, triumph, and the trials of life. Jenny shared how her family had wanted her to move back to Houston after Rob's death but she resisted, knowing that the best thing she could do for Billy and herself was to find healing in the very place where she had been wounded.

"Wow, what a statement," I thought to myself. There's really no other place you can be healed. Maybe Shirley was right to build a new tradition with just her and JD on the foundation of the old traditions. Reality doesn't change to meet our desires; we must change to meet reality.

I enjoyed the game but I must admit, I enjoyed the conversation a lot more. She knew exactly what I was feeling inside and often finished my sentences. She was more than willing to confront me when I gave a vague or elusive response. This didn't bother me, as I feel like she has a right to challenge me because of her own experience with pain.

I dropped everyone off at their homes, safe and sound, and headed toward my house. This had indeed been a unique day. As I walked through the back door, the first thing that caught my eye was my journal, lying on the table. I opened it up to the next blank page and wrote this title across the top: Iron Sharpens Iron.

What lessons had I learned today?

- Everyone has pain but not everyone has progress.
- Pain really does produce gain.
- There are lessons to be learned every day in life.
- Life is a process, not an event.
- Love demands confrontation and not just confirmation.
- The master's hand is always involved.
- Sparks can be a sign of progress.

I marked it up as a great day. I lived, I laughed, and I learned. I captured all of my thoughts in this one sentence: The rewards of life are truly worth the journey. I think I'll sleep on that one.

Chapter 6

Bearing the Marks

The winter winds howled at my window like a starving wolf as I awoke to a cold, December morning. It's now only twenty-one days away from Christmas—where has this year gone? As I pulled back the curtain, it was easy to see that winter was rapidly leaving its mark on the terrain; not a single leaf hung from any of the trees. The mountaintops were covered with a skiff of snow. Though still two full weeks before it's officially winter, for all practical purposes, it was here!

My progress on the project is moving right along. Working at nights all week, I was able to gold plate it. It looked amazing! I believe the contrast between the silver handle and the golden blade was going to make this sword special and unique. I could hardly wait to see it all assembled, but first things first. Next on the agenda, I must get the blade engraved.

I have an appointment with Max to do the engraving on the sword. But we actually had a meeting at ten o'clock at Jerry's Restaurant beforehand. This would give me an opportunity to talk to him about the service last Sunday. I was shocked that he took me up on my offer. He was in quite a hurry after service so we didn't get time to visit. I hoped to do that today.

I had just enough time to read my devotion. The time crunch got me rolling. The sweet smell of coffee wafted into my bedroom, announcing its presence, and I was more than ready for my first cup!

Sitting down with my coffee, I opened my devotional to

December 4. Today's story was about a young boy from a remote Polynesian island and the pain that he had to experience to be considered a man. This story first broke on the National Geographic television program called "Taboo." It centered on the cultural practice of tattooing. In this particular tribe, the young men have to be tattooed over ninety percent of their bodies without making a sound or reacting to their pain. This process actually takes several days. Often the young men's pain can cause them to go in and out of shock and has even resulted in death. But if they can endure to the end, they will be considered ready to face the difficulties of life without relenting or drawing back.

The chief uses a primitive instrument that looks more like a wood chisel than a modern-day tattoo needle. He dips the jagged edge in the dye and taps it with a rod to break the skin and deposit the dye beneath. This process must be repeated thousands of times until the pattern covers his legs, stomach, back, arms, chest, etc. When it's completed, the young boy actually looks as if he is wearing an ink suit. In fact, all of the men of the tribe only wear a loin cloth. The rest of their body carries the marks of this moment for the rest of their lives.

The writer ends the devotion by sharing how life itself can mark us with scars that sometimes stand out to others as the tattoos on this young man. Even though we try our best to hide them, no one but God can take away the pain within.

As I close the journal, I began to reflect concerning the scars in my own life and how things have marked me not only for this life but also for eternity. Some of them God will heal, but others will remain behind. They will become the badge of honor commemorating a particular moment too sacred to forget.

The greatest thing about the whole story is the fact that the young boy's father cradles this child's head in his lap throughout the entire process. He never leaves the boy alone regardless of the pain he encounters. Such a beautiful picture is painted here of our heavenly Father who has promised to never leave us nor forsake us. He is our constant companion even in the midst of our pain.

The clock on the wall clicked along and I did not want to be late. As I opened up the back door, the north wind cut through me like a knife. I couldn't get to the truck fast enough this morning. It made me wish I had warmed up the truck ahead of time, but even in its cold state it was warm in contrast to the wind outside.

As I pulled up to Jerry's Restaurant, I saw Max's truck parked near the front door. I stepped inside and scanned the crowd to see where Max sat. I found him in the corner booth, wearing a Levi jacket with a sheep-lined collar. But it was the cowboy hat that was the dead giveaway. I greeted the gang as I made my way across the room.

"Howdy," Max said, as I took my seat.

I said, "Hey," as I noticed Jenny out of the corner of my eye coming out of the kitchen. She signaled with her hand that she would come to our table in just a minute. "Well, Max. I wanted to thank you for visiting our church last week. I hope you enjoyed the service."

"Yep, you were right. We felt right at home. Peggy liked it, too. The people took us in like two drifters on a cattle drive."

About that time, Jenny walked up and said, "Happy Birthday, birthday boy!" I could feel the heat rush to my face as Max looked me right in the eyes.

"Thank you Ma'am," I replied as a smile creased across my face. "Max, this is Jenny. Jenny—Max."

Jenny's hand looked as small as a child's as Max's hand consumed hers. "Nice to meet you Jenny," Max said.

Jenny took our orders and headed back to the kitchen. "Pretty girl," Max said. "But apparently, you've already figured that one out on your own."

"What do you mean?" I said desperately trying to hide my feelings.

Max chuckled and said, "This is not my first rodeo, son! I can tell when sparks are flying. After all, you do know I'm a silversmith." A grin came across his weathered face. "Looks like something special is going on."

"You think so?" I questioned.

"Yep. I can tell," he replied.

"How so?"

"Well, life leaves a mark on people and often it shapes them for the next relationship they will encounter. It's apparent to me that both of you have experienced your own pain and that pain has left you with a common ground on which to lay a foundation for your relationship."

"You picked all that up from a hand shake?" I responded.

"Nope. I picked that up from the marks left behind, visible to everybody but you. You know, Chuck, you've got to learn to trust your own heart and to read these marks for yourself. You see, her hard knocks have left her with a tender heart. That don't happen to everybody."

"Well, guys. Breakfast is served," Jenny said as she set everything down on the table. "Don't eat too much," she winked at me. "You need to save room for your birthday dinner tonight."

"Believe me, I will. It's not every day that I get to eat a home cooked meal."

"Enjoy your meal, guys," as she turned to walk away, my eyes following her all the way to the kitchen door.

When I turned back toward Max, I noticed that he had already removed his cowboy hat and bowed his head. He said, "Shall we bless the meal?" I nodded and to my surprise, he began to pray. "Good Lord, we want to thank you for another day. Regardless of the cold weather, help us to make the most of it. Thank you for your bounty and for all your blessings. Amen."

I was taken aback by the whole event but I tried to act normal as we made eye contact. He gently smiled and began to eat his meal. I was eating too, but my mind was working overtime. I was thinking about that young man on a small island in the South Pacific and how it must have taken his entire life to discover what he had gained from his painful moment that somehow made him into a man.

It was becoming more apparent to me that I have wasted a lot of time ignoring the obvious lessons I should have learned. Even so, God has never stopped trying to teach me and He has brought a new teacher to my table. There was just something about Max that intrigued me. I found myself constantly wondering what was going on inside his head that's covered with his calm resolve. He just might have the keys to unlock my pain. One thing is certain: He's a lot closer to God than I originally thought he was and now I was uncertain who's helping whom.

When Jenny returned to the table with the bill, I felt her gentle touch on my shoulder reassuring me, as if to say, "Everything is going to be all right."

Max grabbed the ticket out of her hand and with a smile on his face, said, "I'll take care of the birthday boy's breakfast; you can handle his supper!" They both chuckled at my expense as I fought off the embarrassment.

I spoke up and said, "I'll cover the tip; the service has been extra special this morning."

Jenny smiled as she turned to walk away. "I'll see you around six o'clock!"

She turned back and nodded and waved. I hustled to join Max at the counter and we walked out together. I told him I would follow him to the shop. He instructed me to pull around back. Once inside the shop, Max turned up the heat and asked to see the sword blade. I began to unwrap it from the Styrofoam packaging and rolled out the blade. You could see Max's eyes light up as he said, "My, what a canvas we have to begin with. What do you have in mind?"

"Luke 6:40," I responded. "The student, when fully trained, will become like his teacher."

"That's good!" Max responded. "I really like it! Now let's get some measurements so I can set the machine."

"Machine?" I questioned.

"Oh yeah. There is very little free hand done nowadays. Computers have affected us all. We've become victims of the industrial age. Yep. It looks like it will fit fine on here. We've got room for the scripture and the scroll around it. That will be a great addition!"

"Do you think it will be too busy?"

"I don't think so," he responded. "I can show you what it looks like before we start."

"Really?"

"Yep. It's amazing what you can do with the right equipment. Well, do you approve?" he asked, after setting it all up.

"I reckon I do. It looks perfect with the silver scroll and scripture against the golden background! Let it roll!"

I watched through the glass as the machine strategically etched out our dream on the metal blade, adding beauty with every stroke. Change was underway. The beauty added outweighed the loss of the metal being cut away. Apparently, it always does. Romans 8:28 came to mind—all things do work together for the good of them that love God, who are the called according to His purpose. I was getting a ringside seat for this performance.

"Something's on my mind, Max."

"Well, it's a little late for that now!" he replied.

"Oh, I'm not talking about the blade."

"Then what are you talking about?"

"To be honest, I'd like to spend more time with you."

"Go on," Max said. "I'm listening."

"I was wondering if you'd like to join me on this project."

"Are you sure you want me to?" he said. "I know this is very special to you."

"Yeah, I think I would, if you would consider doing it."

There was a long pause. Then Max responded, "Under one condition."

"What's that?" I replied.

"That you lead the project and I work for you!"

With hesitation, I said, "Alright. I'm not really sure I'm qualified to lead you."

He smiled and said, "Oh, believe me. I won't hold back my feelings nor my opinion!"

He stuck out his hand and I said, "OK. It's a deal then." And we shook on it.

About that time, the machine began to beep, signaling us that the job was completed. Max slid back the door and removed the blade. It nearly took away my breath as he held the blade up with both hands. It was absolutely perfect! Max hit the buffing wheel and polished the blade till it shone like a new dime.

"Well, what do I owe you, Max?"

"Owe me?" he responded. "I thought we were partners. If I'm a partner, I have to invest the same as you. Call me when you're ready to meet again."

"One more thing, Max, before I leave."

"What's that, son?"

"Is it OK if I just drop by from time to time even if we're not working on the project?"

"You're always welcome here."

"Thanks, Max."

"You bet, Chuck. Now remember what I told you: Trust your heart and learn to read the marks of life."

"I'll do my best and I'll talk to you soon." With that word of advice, I headed out the door. As I climbed in the truck, all I could think about was how this was shaping up to be my best birthday in the last twenty years. Guess I'd better head home and get ready for tonight. I feel a lot more comfortable about it after getting Max's viewpoint on the situation. He seems to see things a lot more clearly than I do, even about my own life.

As I walked into the house, I laid the blade on the counter and began to unwrap it again. I was totally blown away by how perfect it looked. In fact, I was blown away by the whole process. Nothing happened like I thought it would, yet everything exceeded my expectations.

I took one last glance in the rearview mirror as I pulled up to Jenny's house. My nerves were on edge, but I wasn't sure why. It's not like I was afraid of Jenny, she's exceptionally kind. To be honest, I was a little afraid of myself and what I might be hiding deep inside.

I cleared my throat as I rang the doorbell. Jenny stunned me as she answered the door. Boy, she looked terrific!

"Come on in, Chuck. Make yourself at home."

Billy was sitting on the couch playing with his DS. "Hey, Billy."

"Hi Uncle Chuck. I guess it's ok if I call you Uncle Chuck. That's what JD calls you."

"Sure. That will be fine for now," I responded.

"Boy, something really smells good," I said, as I laid my coat across the back of the couch.

"It's pork roast with potatoes and carrots. I understand that is your favorite," Jenny said.

"Where did you get that information?" I asked.

Jenny said, "Well, let's just say a little birdie named Shirley told me."

"So you girls have been talking behind my back. What else should I know?"

Jenny smiled. "That's enough for now I guess. Are you really hungry?"

"Yep, I sure am. I haven't eaten anything since breakfast. My appetite might just be an embarrassment to me tonight."

"No way! You are safe around here. I like cooking for people that are really hungry. I just hate to put forth all the effort and have someone pick around in their food like a bird."

"There's no bird here," I replied. "Maybe a vulture!"

"Well, good," she said. "Everything is ready; let's gather around the table. Billy, do you want to say the blessing?"

"Sure, Mom. Dear Jesus, thank you for the food. And thank you for Uncle Chuck and for all that he has done for JD and me. May this be the best birthday he has ever had. In Jesus' name. Amen."

"Thank you, Billy. I believe it might just be."

We all began to eat. "Wow! This is even better than it smells. It's really good, Jenny."

"Oops," she said as she jumped to her feet. "I almost forgot the crescent rolls in the oven." Jenny removed them from the oven with a well-used potholder and set them on top of the stove.

"Crescent rolls too?" I exclaimed. "What are you trying to do, fatten me up for the kill?"

"A good meal won't hurt anything every now and then," as she made her way back to the table.

"Thanks so much, Jenny. I really appreciate this more than you will ever know." And I truly did.

She patted my arm and said, "I know you do, Chuck. We also appreciate what you have done for us lately."

Conversation continued as I indulged in one of the finest meals I'd had in a long time. Sitting around her table was as natural as sitting around my own.

"I'd better stop for now," I said. "I'm about to blow up."

"Not yet," Jenny replied. "There's still a birthday cake to go."

"I'm going to have to wait on that for just a little while." I began to pick up my plate and head to the sink.

"No, Chuck," she insisted. "I will clean up later. Let's go in the living room and find a better chair to sit in."

Billy piped up, "Mom, do you care if I go play some video games in my room?"

"That'll be fine," she said. "But only until ten o'clock."

"OK," he responded, bouncing up the steps. "See you in a little while, Uncle Chuck." I nodded in reply.

"That Max is quite a character, Chuck," Jenny observed.

"You can say that again; one of the most interesting people I have ever met."

"What makes him so interesting?" Jenny quizzed.

"I don't know, Jenny. He's like the eye of a hurricane. You know he's had his share of trouble but yet, nothing seems to rattle him."

"I can see what you are talking about. I felt the same way when I shook his hand. And brother, what a hand!"

"Yeah, I know!" We both chuckled together. "Guess what he said about us."

"What?"

"He said that both of us have been shaped by the same pain."

"Wow! He got all of that from just shaking my hand?"

"No, I don't think so. I don't think it has anything to do with it. He's just able to read people like no one else I've ever seen."

"What else did he say?"

I hesitated. "I don't know if I should say."

"You've got to say. You can't just leave me hanging."

"Well, to be honest, he said that we have something special here and that I should learn to trust my heart."

Jenny reached to grab my hand. "Really, Chuck. What do you think?"

"I don't know Jenny. I really care a lot about you but I think you deserve so much more. To tell you the truth, I'm afraid of what I can give. I'm damaged merchandise, you know."

"We're all damaged Chuck. You don't live for forty years and not experience battle scars."

"I know but you have done an amazing job handling your pain while raising Billy. I, on the other hand, have just closed off from the whole world."

"But Chuck, you're just forty-three years old today. There's still a lot of time for you to be healed and experience happiness."

"You think so?"

"I know so! Now, let's have a piece of this Red Velvet Cake."

"Red Velvet! That's my favorite!"

"Really!"

"I surrender!" I said. "Between you and Shirley, I don't have a chance anyway!"

We talked and laughed as we ate our cake and drank our coffee, exchanging stories from our past, many of them marked by scars that we still carry today.

"I guess I'd better call it a night," I sighed. "Thanks for a wonderful meal and even greater conversation."

"I'll walk you out," she said as she handed me my coat.

We walked toward the driveway, hand in hand. "I really feel lucky to have you in my life at this time. You seem like an answer to my prayers."

"So are you, Chuck. Happy Birthday!" She turned and kissed

me on the cheek. As we embraced, something happened that I didn't expect. I began to weep. It was like a dam had broken inside of me. She stood there silently, holding me in her arms as I cried. Finally, I was able to contain my emotions. I apologized, not really knowing what to say. She assured me that everything was fine. I kissed her softly and left.

What a day it had been. It felt like my first birthday, instead of my forty-third. I walked in the house and picked up my journal from the table. Plopping down in my recliner, I searched for the next blank page, titling today's entry with these three simple words: Bearing the Marks. What have I learned?

- Life can and will mark you.
- Not all marks are negative.
- We can learn to minister out of our pain.
- God is touched by what touches us.
- Release is necessary for restoration.
- It's never too late to move forward.
- Every new day is an opportunity for a new birth.

I lifted both hands toward heaven and said, "Thank you Lord for surrounding me with loving people that I can love and live life with today, tomorrow, and forever. And thank you for making this birthday the happiest of all."

Chapter 7

Getting a Handle on Life

I woke one Saturday morning to bitter conditions outside. In fact, the highest temperature was predicted to only be in the teens with wind chills in the single digits. Christmas was only a week away and the year was quickly coming to an end. It has been a year laced with change, where often I felt like I had lost my grip. Yet in another way, it seemed to be coming together without my assistance at all. Maybe I've been the problem all along!

I'm coming to discover that it matters who's in control. Changing control from our hands to God's hands can turn our circumstance completely around and enable us to get a handle on life.

I had a full day in store: A meeting with Max in the morning to work on the project and Christmas shopping in the afternoon. Plus, Jenny and I had a date scheduled that evening. I really looked forward to being with her again. Our relationship is continuing to develop. We were making big plans since both of our families were coming in the following week. I nervously looked forward to meeting her parents; I certainly hoped they approve of me. I know how deeply they loved Rob.

Jenny says she's also nervous about meeting Landon and Rachel and their families, but I'm sure they will be more than thrilled with her since they've pushed me for over twenty years to find somebody and move on with my life. I thought about telling them that I was in a relationship, but I decided to surprise them instead. It may be their greatest Christmas present. It will at least allow them to focus on something else.

Well, enough speculating about next week; I needed to get this day started. I realize a little more every day what a creature of habit I am. I grabbed my coffee, picked up my devotional, and sat down in my recliner. Twenty years of living by myself has shaped my schedule. But now I began to wonder what my future might be!

As I opened my devotional, apparently the disciples were pondering the same question. My Saturday's story came from Matthew, chapter 20, as the mother of James and John, the sons of Zebedee, approaches Jesus with this question, "Can my sons sit on your left and right when you enter your kingdom?"

Jesus answers, "You know not what you ask for." Then He poses to them two pertinent questions: "Are you able to drink of the cup that I drink of? Are you able to be baptized with the baptism that I shall be baptized with?"

Totally perplexed, they quickly respond to Jesus that they were able. I'm sure their answer was based on what they thought would happen, yet, they had no idea of what was coming.

Life is full of twists and turns and only God knows the future. Jesus chooses this awkward moment to teach the principles of Kingdom life. He begins by saying, "Some things are in God's hands alone and only time will reveal His will." His ways are not our ways; therefore, we will never be able to figure it out. That's where faith comes in. We must trust the Master. He ends His lesson by telling them that the greatest joy is found in serving. It is the kingdom way of advancement.

As I laid down my devotional, I wondered just how much of my life has been spent in serving others. Suddenly, Johnny enters my mind. He was such a powerful example of a servant. It's as if the whole text I'd just read was written about him, especially verse 27, "And whosoever will be chief among you, let him be your servant." It was clear to see how Johnny had become chief of the fire department, it was through a life of faithful service.

When all is said and done, there appears to be only two categories of people: those who serve and those who enjoy being served. Unfortunately, I fall into that second category. For over twenty years, I've been the one receiving service. Yet, I believe somehow that God is calling me out of that position to serve those around me. Like the disciples, I'm not sure I know what I'm doing. Regardless, change is still underway!

Max was waiting. I wasn't really sure how much I'd be able to help him. He's the master when it comes to forging silver, and that's what needed to be done. I could at least bring him breakfast and keep him company. I told him I would run by Dairy Queen and pick up some sausage and biscuits. That would have to do us both this chilly morning. He seemed to be happy about it. He really doesn't like to eat out much; he feels more comfortable in his shop or on his ranch.

With my errand ran, I pulled up in front of the shop and headed inside. His truck was parked in its normal spot; I have no idea how long he has been here. I always feel like I'm catching up when I am around him anyway.

The back door is closed tight to hold in the precious heat. So I made my way in the front door, hollering, "Hey," as I enter. He quickly responds from the shop to come on back.

"Are you ready for a sausage biscuit?" I shouted.

"I reckon I am," he responded. "I've been here since 5 AM putting the finishing touches on a few things for Christmas. I love making my gifts; they seem to mean a little more when there's a little sweat involved."

I agreed and smiled with a nod. "Let's take a break now and eat these biscuits before they get cold."

Max removed his cowboy hat and I knew what was coming next. But he asked me to offer thanks this morning. I did and we began to talk or should I say, I began to talk; Max always seems to leave the conversation up to me.

"Max, what is your view of servanthood?"

He swallowed hard and responded, "What's got you thinking about that, son?"

"Well, to be honest, my devotion this morning was about Jesus and his disciples. They were looking for a position but Jesus was calling servants."

I hushed, hoping that he would respond. After a long pause, he did, hitting the nail right on the head. "It's really about who you live for: others or yourself."

Wow-that stung! "Yep. I'm coming to the same conclusion, Max."

"Sounds like you're on the right track, son." He crumpled up his wrapper and threw it in the trash. "You about ready to get started?" he said.

"I suppose so."

"What are we doing today?" he asked.

"I guess our objective is to get a handle on this sword."

He chuckled and then replied, "It's kind of useless without one, that's for sure! What do you have in mind?"

"I was thinking about turning this into the handle," as I opened the box revealing a piece of silver, six inches wide and a quarter inch thick, measuring about a foot long. "I'm sure this is going to be too much for the job but it's always better to have too much than too little."

He picked up the piece of silver and began caressing it in his hand as if it were a baby. I could tell by the way he handled it that he was the master and he could already see the potential of what he was touching. He began to fire the metal, turning with precision to keep it evenly heated. His pliers looked like an extension of his fingers; it was easy to see that he had done this a thousand times.

I watched with great anticipation of what would happen next. He picked up a strange looking hammer and began to hit the silver. It was then for the first time that I noticed the grooves in the top of the anvil. They held the silver in place like a cradle, allowing him to change the shape with every blow.

My mind was flooded with thoughts as I sat there in silence. One thought seemed to stand out above the others; if we can just get in groove with the Master, He already has a plan in mind to bring beauty out of our ashes. The problem is we are often like the disciples; we have our own agenda that is preventing us from the beauty He has in mind.

Back and forth he went from the fire to the anvil, from the anvil to the fire, handling the hammer and the pliers like a skilled musician with a plan that was known only sketched in his own mind. Therefore, only he could bring about what he had visualized for this silver bar. Every blow of the hammer brought the handle more in focus as the metal was shaped and curved to fit the sword.

This process went on for over two hours as sweat coursed down Max's face. This, my friend, was a true labor of love!

Finally, Max broke the silence as he wiped the sweat from his forehead. "You have a decision that you need to make, Chuck."

"What is it?" I said.

"Do you want me to leave the hammer marks or do you want them smoothed away?"

"I'm not sure," I responded. "What do you think?"

Once again, he wiped his face with his bandana. "Well, to be honest, I kinda like to leave the hammer marks. It reminds me of the whole process."

"I agree," I said. "Let's leave them. They will be a reminder for life."

"We still have a little work that we will need to do. I still need to tap out the end for the pommel, bore out the other end to attach the blade and the hilt. But that's a one-man job if you need to go. What's on your plate today, Chuck?"

"Well, I'm going Christmas shopping. And Jenny and I have a date tonight."

"Really!" he said as a smile creased his face. "How's it going with you two?"

"Pretty good, I think. We talk for hours every night. And we keep discovering that we have more and more in common."

"Is that so?" he said with a chuckle.

"I know, you told me that weeks ago. But I'm just discovering it for myself!"

"Well, I didn't say a thing, Chuck."

"Let me ask you something."

"What is it?"

"Any suggestions on what I might buy them for Christmas?"

"As for Jenny, I think I'd better steer clear of that one. But as for that boy of hers, I think he needs a horse."

"A horse?" I shouted. "Are you joking? I live in town and so does Jenny. Where in the world would we keep a horse?"

"How about my ranch?" he quickly responded.

"You're serious, aren't you?" I quickly retorted. "I don't know if Jenny would be for that or not!"

"You never know till you ask." He smiled as he took a drink of his coffee.

"Don't you think maybe he's a little young for a horse?"

"No, I don't think so," he says. "He needs a foal that he can grow up with. He'll learn a lot of lessons from the horse. And Jenny might not be as much against it as you think she will be."

"But I wouldn't even know how to begin to pick out a horse."

"You get the permission," he said as he touched my shoulder. "I'll get the horse."

"It's a deal," I responded. "I'll let you know if I can get Jenny on our side!"

With that I left the shop, a little more overwhelmed than I had entered. This Christmas is shaping up to be a doozy! I'm already a little overcome by the emotions that this time of year seems to resurface. Sometimes I struggle just to ward off panic attacks, especially since today is the anniversary of the fire that took Susie and Lizzie away from me.

Though years have taken away the pain, the guilt remains and I find myself retracing every step and asking the same question over and over—What could I have done to avert this tragedy? I discover each time that it is more than an effort in futility because nothing can bring them back. I know I must learn to turn the page and begin a new chapter. One thing is certain—the last thing I want to do is go Christmas shopping alone. I think I'll call Jenny and make the day of it.

The phone rings and rings, I'm expecting a voice mail when finally, I hear her voice. It's like an anchor for my heart in the midst of the storm.

"Hi Jen. What's up with you today?"

"Nothing much," she said. "Just getting home from grocery shopping. Had my hands full and couldn't reach the phone."

"Yeah, I was wondering if you were going to answer."

"Well, Chuck, I've sure been busy since my feet hit the floor this morning. But I can see the fruit of my labor; the house is clean, the laundry is done, I dropped Billy off at JD's because they're having a sleepover at his house with a few boys from the troop, and I'm planning to spend the day relaxing. What's up with you?"

"Not much," I said. "I've just finished working with Max this morning. Or maybe I should say, watching Max work. But I was thinking about driving up to Meadowwood Mall and do a little Christmas shopping. Would you be willing to give up your relaxing for that?"

"Absolutely," she responded. "That sounds like a blast! Give me around 30 minutes and I should be ready to go."

"You bet," I said. "I'll see you in thirty."

Suddenly I felt like someone had thrown me a life preserver and started pulling me from my past. A glance at my watch showed it was already nearly one o'clock. I had just enough time to grab a snack. I'd get something light; that way we could get something to eat together if she hasn't had lunch.

I ordered a six piece McNuggets and a small coke from the McDonald's drive-thru line and took it home so I could freshen up a little, though I hadn't done anything to make me even break a sweat. I just watched Max work. Hustling around, I gave the truck a once over to make sure it was presentable before I picked Jenny up.

The truck was warm and toasty and so was I. I felt like I did twenty years ago with emotions bouncing back and forth, being rekindled like a fire. I couldn't even sort out my feelings, much less express them. Could it be that I was falling in love? I knew this for sure: I enjoyed being with her more and more and being by myself less and less. I hoped Jenny's feelings were mutual. I'd been content to stay in my pain for twenty years and ignore life completely. Now, however, I desired things to move along, though what laid before me scared me more than a little.

At Jenny's, I left the truck running with the heat on high. She met me at the door, bundled up like an Eskimo.

"Are you cold?" I said.

"Not anymore," she chuckled, as we hurried to the truck.

The door handle was frozen. I tried several times to open it, but with no results, so we ran around to my side. She hopped in but stayed in the middle. I was happy with this decision and jumped in myself and closed the door. We buckled up and started out of the driveway.

"I think I'll give Shirley a call and let her know of the change of our plans."

"OK," I said as I listened to one side of the phone call.

"Hi Shirley. Chuck and I are going to run up to Reno and do some Christmas shopping. How are the boys getting along?"

After a long pause, Jenny responded, "OK. If you need us, give us a call. I'll have my phone with me. Bye bye."

"What did she say?" I questioned.

"She said that the boys are having a blast. And told us to have fun."

"Well, first things first. Are you hungry?" I asked.

"No, Billy and I had lunch before I took him to JD's. But I'd love to have a hot chocolate to thaw out my bones. It seems like that kind of day!"

I pull through Starbucks and picked up our hot chocolate before we headed north.

"Thanks for joining me today, Jenny. I just didn't want to do Christmas shopping alone."

"Believe me, that's no problem," she responded. "I'm always ready to go shopping and this will give me a chance to pick up some things for Billy and my parents as well."

"That's good," I said. "And hopefully, you can help me finish my shopping list. I usually just give money. I hate to shop so bad! I guess it's a man thing. Max told me this morning that he makes all his gifts. It sure made me think about the money thing being so impersonal."

"Did y'all have a good time together?" she asked, interrupting my rambling.

"You bet!" I responded. "I enjoy every moment with him. I think it's because I never know what he's going to say next. You'll never guess what he suggested this morning."

"What?" she asked with a puzzled look on her face.

"You'd better brace yourself for this one. You are buckled up, aren't you?" I said with a chuckle.

"Tell me," she said. "I'm ready."

"He suggested that I buy Billy a horse for Christmas!"

"A horse!" she exclaimed. Her voice gave up the fact that she was totally in shock! "You can't do that, Chuck. That's expensive, way too expensive!"

"Being expensive is all you're worried about? I expected you to freak out about it being a horse! With questions like: Where are we going to keep him? How are we going to care for him? I don't care about the money part."

"Well, where would we keep him?" she questioned. "Now that you have brought it up."

"Max said we could keep him on his ranch. That he would care for him along with the rest of his livestock. We could help with the hay and Billy could ride him anytime he wanted. What do you think?"

"I'm not really certain," she said. "I don't know. What do you think?"

"It's your decision, Jenny."

"I guess it's OK," she said. "I'll do my best to help you any way I can but we're moving in uncharted waters as far as I'm concerned!"

"I would say that was an understatement! I'll tell you what I'll do, I'll help Billy with the horse if you'll help me with Christmas shopping. What do you say?"

"It's a deal!" she said reaching into her purse to retrieve paper and pen. Then she asked, "Who all do we need to buy for?"

"Everyone, basically," I responded. I don't even know where to begin. I've got Rachel and John, Ethan and Emily, Landon, and Renee. I don't buy for their boys anymore since they haven't come for Christmas in years. There's Shirley and JD and of course, you!" That brought a smile to her face. "And I was thinking about getting something for your mom and dad. Maybe a picture of you and Billy, nicely framed. Do you think they would like that?"

"Absolutely!" she responded. "They are grandparents. They like anything with Billy in it. I'm sure they're not expecting anything from you."

"I know. But I thought it would be a friendly gesture. Or maybe a peace offering."

"You silly thing!" she said rocking her shoulder into mine. "They're going to love you."

"I hope so," I said. "I want to get off on the right foot!"

"Since you've brought that up, should I buy something for your family?" she questioned.

"Heavens, no! The simple fact that we are dating and that you're helping to bring me out of my cave will be gift enough for them. They will probably nominate you for the Congressional Medal of Honor! And I know they are going to love you to pieces. And Billy, too. Finally, Ethan will have someone to hang out with and he won't be bored stiff at Uncle Chuck's. Are you nervous about meeting each other's families, Jenny?"

"Kinda," she responded. "Just because they are going to know that we are serious about our relationship. How about you?" she quizzed.

"Well, sure," I said. "But it's more about my insecurities. I feel awkward in almost every social situation after being closed off for so many years."

"You'll be fine," she said as she patted me on the arm and leaned her head on my shoulder. "You don't appear to be awkward at all, and I'll be right there by your side."

"You'd better be," I responded with a smile and a glance her way.

"Well, there's Meadowwood Mall ahead," she said. "Are you ready for this?"

"You bet!" I replied. Hand in hand for the next few hours we went from store to store checking off our gift lists. I can truthfully say that the very thing I dreaded for weeks was turning out to be the most enjoyable day ever.

Returning back to Fallon, our conversation, however, took a more serious note as we began talking about our future together. Jenny asked a question, "What do we do to make this holiday season different from the past?"

"What do you mean?" I questioned.

"Well, I know today is the anniversary of the fire. And I know that we are just days away from the anniversary of Rob's death as well. It seems like to me that we are continually allowing our past to rob us of our future happiness."

"What you are saying is true, Jenny. But I just thought this was our lot in life. I didn't know we would have an opportunity to change our situation."

"I know that is true, Chuck. But we can change our focus. Just like today. We focused on Christmas shopping. This has caused you to change your normal thinking. Right?"

"Yep!" I responded. "But we can't shop every day for the next few weeks!"

"I'm not saying that, you silly thing! But we can get a game plan together to focus on something besides ourselves."

"That's strange you should say that, Jenny. I've been thinking about the same thing today. What's your plan?"

With a smile on her face, she responded, "I think we should look for opportunities to serve our community. That way we'll focus on other people instead of ourselves."

"I'm game if you are! There's got to be something we could do. I'd like to make a suggestion. The anniversary of Rob's death is January 9th. Why don't we take Billy and JD to see the Kraft Hunger Bowl Game at AT&T Park in San Francisco? It would be great for them and I believe it will help you cope as well. But you'll have to help me talk Shirley into letting JD go. She's holding on pretty tight to him since Johnny's death."

"I don't think that will be a big problem," Jenny said. "It's a deal!"

We sealed our deal with a quick kiss instead of a handshake as I pulled up in her driveway. I could not believe how one day could change so much concerning my past.

I helped her unload her stuff, kissed her good-night, and headed home. I headed straight for my journal that, over the last few weeks, had become my progress chart. Opening to the next blank page I wrote this title: Getting a Handle on Life. What had I learned today?

- Nothing can change the past.
- The past can rob you of your future.
- Nothing changes until your focus does.
- Life is best lived in the present.
- Change always involves planning and effort.
- Fulfillment comes from serving others.
- Investing in others is the only way to recoup personal loss.

It had indeed been a day of new beginnings. I am glad to say that I was ready to leave the past behind and embrace the future. I'm so thankful for a new perspective; after all these years, I feel like I was beginning to get a grip on life again.

Chapter 8

Finding Balance/Bringing Closure

The shrill of my alarm clock made me sit straight up in the bed like a soldier responding to reveille. To be honest, I hadn't had a good sleep. I was afraid that I might oversleep and I couldn't afford to do that, least of all on this particular day! I had a ton of things to do before we started our road trip.

It was January 9, 2011—a day we'd all been waiting for. The Wolf Pack was playing in the Kraft Hunger Bowl in San Francisco. AT&T Stadium I'm sure would be packed to capacity as we take on Boston College. And we plan to be there, rooting the Wolf Pack to victory! Bowl games are a rarity in our division. Therefore, almost everyone in Fallon would be heading west today. Jenny and I were taking the boys. JD and Billy haven't talked about anything else since Christmas Day. But before we could leave, I needed to get the oil changed in Jenny's SUV, make sure that everything is road ready, fill it with gas, and decorate it with Wolf Pack flags and stickers lest anyone in California mistake us for Eagles fans!

It was a time-saving blessing that I wouldn't have to drive out to Shirley's to pick up JD. He'd been staying with Jenny since Thursday night. Shirley had a doctor's appointment on Friday morning in Ely. JD's father, Shirley and Johnny's son Jonathan, was incarcerated there, and she wanted to stop by and bring him some encouragement. She knows things are more emotionally difficult around the holidays for him.

I can't even imagine how it would feel being stuck in prison and unable to even wrap his arms around his son. Especially since JD is growing up and pulling away all at the same time. I believe the visit will be good for both of them. She'll be staying with Renee and Landon, which would give them a chance to visit as well. And most of all, she won't have to worry about how JD is doing for the weekend. Our great plan was coming together.

With a cup of coffee in hand, I reached beside my chair to retrieve my daily devotional and turn to today's date. The story I read is about Nikolas (Nik) Wallenda, an acrobatic aerialist and daredevil, born on January 24, 1979. Nik represents the seventh generation born to the Flying Wallendas, which traces back to the 1700s. Nik, however, had no desire to follow in the family business. He wanted to be a medical doctor. But as fate would have it, he felt a calling from his past that would shape his future.

In his own words, he described that he could not allow the death of his grandfather, Karl, to go down in the record books as a failure. You see, Karl Wallenda, had trained for years to walk between two skyscrapers in Puerto Rico but his attempt ended in tragedy as he plunged to his death. This had occurred less than a year before Nik's birth; therefore, he felt compelled to take up his mantle. So at age nineteen, his pursuit began. Over the last thirteen years, Nik prepared for one moment in time slated for June 10, 2011, where he would attempt to walk the tight wire at the very place that took the life of his grandfather. He has just finished his "Walk Across America" tour, completing similar walks in ten different cities. This is rather unique since the number ten means "test."

This story ends with one of the most powerful statements ever heard, coming from Nik himself: "If I can keep my balance, I can bring closure for my family, put history to bed once and for all, and open a doorway for future generations." Wow! What a powerful statement.

As I closed my devotional, I felt salty tears roll down my face. Something about this story struck a deep chord within me that made me wonder if this type of closure was possible in my own life. I, too, need to find my balance and close the door on my history that keeps robbing me of my future.

Once out of the shower, I headed across town to meet Max at the shop. I must keep my eyes on the clock if I expected to get everything accomplished and out of town by noon. The game starts at six o'clock, and we want to be sure and have plenty of time; we don't want to miss a thing!

Pulling up in front of the shop, I see Max's truck loaded with hay sitting in its familiar spot. As I entered, I heard the polishing wheel spinning away; Max was at it working and didn't even hear the bell ring. So I made my way on to the back. He caught a glimpse of me out of the corner of his eye and hit the switch on the machine. He turned to me with a big smile.

"Just in time, Chuck! I wanted you to see the finished product," he said, as he held out the handle guard like an offering. It was breathtaking!

"Well, what do you think?" he inquired.

"It looks amazing!" I exclaimed as the light danced off of every curve and curl like a sparkling diamond. "I can hardly recognize it with all the filigree work you have done on it. This must have taken you hours!"

"I didn't keep up with the time," he replied. "I was much more intrigued with the outcome. Doing filigree work always reminds me of life. There's some parts of life that seem to be missing, yet, there's always enough that connects together that reflect His beauty to encourage us to keep going on."

"I love it!" I said. "It speaks to where I am right now because I am trying to put the pieces of my life together, dealing with my past as I plan my future. By the way, what's up with all the hay on your truck?"

"I decided to go by the barn this morning and pick up a load. Gotta make sure the livestock have plenty to eat…. especially since I have another mouth to feed!" he said with a chuckle.

"How is Blaze doing?" I enquired.

"Let me tell you, that's one spunky little filly!" he said, giving me a thumbs up. "She's a real beaute! But she is stubborn as a mule with plenty yet to learn!"

"Well, do I owe you anything?" I asked.

"Nope," he responded. "She doesn't eat much at this stage. I hardly know she's on the place. We're just getting to know each other and every day is a mystery. Billy sure seemed happy to meet her and I love the fact that he named her Blaze! That boy has got a real eye for horses to notice the blaze running down her forehead."

"That's all he talks about, Max," I chimed in. "He told me that was his favorite Christmas present of all times. I didn't quite know how to tell him it wasn't my idea!"

A grin creased across Max's face as he winked his eye and replied, "We'll just keep that our little secret. He doesn't have to know everything as long as he grows to love ole Blaze. He's already been out there a time or two and I've enjoyed getting to know the little fella. And Jenny as well. She's quite a keeper, you know!"

"Yep, I know, Max," I replied.

"Well, what's on the agenda for today?" Max said as he wrapped the handle guard in a cloth for safe keeping and laid it on the shelf.

"As I told you Sunday at church, I won't be able to work on the project with you today because I'm taking Jenny and the boys to San Francisco for the ballgame. I'm not really sure what we can get completed in such a short time."

Max turned and looked me straight in the eye as he said again, "All I need to know from you is what's next on the agenda. I'm used to working alone and since Christmas is over, I've got plenty of time on my hands. I'm ready to get started."

"According to the plan, we need to build a pommel for the end of the sword to balance it out. But to be perfectly honest, I don't have a clue on how to do it or what it should look like. Do you have any suggestions?"

Max began to rub his big hands together and grin from ear to ear. "I've got a couple of ideas but I'd really kinda like to keep it to myself right now, if you don't mind. I hope by now you trust me to explore a little bit on my own."

"Trust you! Are you kidding me?" I responded. "You're about the only thing I can trust besides the Lord! I have no clue of where

I am or what I am doing but I do feel guilty leaving you with the work load while I run out to San Francisco and watch a ball game."

"Don't worry about me. I love watching beauty come out of ashes! And after all, you've got some important issues to deal with at this time," he said as he placed his hand on my shoulder.

"I'd better get moving. I've got a bunch of things to do," I said walking toward the door.

"Y'all enjoy yourselves," Max muttered. "I'll see you next week with my surprise!"

"OK, Max, talk to you later!"

With the oil changed and the car full of gas and fully decorated, I pulled up to Jenny's house. I glanced at my watch and saw that it was twelve o'clock on the dot—Perfect! Jenny greeted me at the door with a cup of coffee and a sausage biscuit.

"The boys and I have already eaten a late breakfast," she said. "But I knew you would wake up running and probably not take time to eat. Am I right?"

"You're right," I responded. "And that's why I love you. You're always thinking about the little things that I'm forgetting. Are the boys ready?"

"Ready? Are you kidding? They've about driven me crazy this morning asking me when you are coming. Boys!" she hollered. "Chuck is here!"

Down the steps they bounded, screaming, "Go Wolf Pack!" They went by me like a shot, heading straight for the SUV. Jenny and I picked up the snacks, blankets, cooler, and everything else needed for a road trip. We loaded them in the back of the car and settled in for our first out of town trip together. Suddenly I felt the power of the moment and I questioned myself, "Is this what it feels like to be a family? Man, if so, I think I like it!"

"Well, boys, what did you think about Christmas?"

JD started by saying, "I love, love, love, love my four-wheeler, Uncle Chuck! It's simply the best gift ever! Billy and I rode it all over the farm last weekend. It was a blast!"

Billy interrupted and said, "No, the best gift ever is Blaze! I've never been around horses in my life but Max told me that I was handling Blaze like a real pro! He also let me ride his horse, Grace. She's real gentle and he can control her every move with the slightest whisper. I want to do that with Blaze someday. I really love going out to the ranch, I am learning so much."

Suddenly the conversation took a different turn as the boys took out their DS and began to play games, occasionally warring with each other as boys do, leaving Jenny and me to talk about our time together over the holidays.

Nervously, I asked her, "What's your overall view of Christmas now that you've had time to process with your family? I'm sure that you've talked to them. Let me break the ice by saying that Rachel and Landon seem to love you more than they do me! They told me that if I did anything to mess up this relationship or to hurt you, they would disown me for good!"

"How sweet is that?" Jenny responded. "I just love your entire family. I especially enjoy how they dote over you like you are a five-year-old kid."

"Doting? Is that what you call it? It seems more like Chinese torture to me!" I retorted.

"Come now—it can't be that bad! Especially if they love me the way you say they do," as she laughed, taking hold of my hand.

"Well, I know whose side you're on! Maybe we should stop talking about my family and start talking about what your family thought about me. Have you talked to them since they've been home?" I asked.

"Yeah, I talked to them last Saturday when the boys were riding four-wheelers at Shirley's house."

"Well, go on. What did they say?"

"They really liked you—especially Mom. She was overwhelmed by your thoughtfulness of getting them a portrait made of me and Billy. By the way, she said it was hanging over the mantle and is the centerpiece of the room. Dad didn't say much, but that is natural for him. Mom does the talking for both of them. But if he didn't like you, I'd know about it! He did tell Mom that he was glad Billy had a male role model in his life and he was impressed by the fact that you had bought Billy a horse rather than just giving him money. He thought the horse would keep Billy grounded and teach him responsibility. I also think it was a great idea for us all to eat together on Christmas day and give our families a chance to meet each other. Mom and Rachel seemed to hit it off and I really enjoyed cooking with Ellen and Renee. Renee is an amazing cook! I was shocked to see Dad talking so much with John. I guess their military background and love of government and politics set the stage for developing a relationship. It was a real hoot to get to know Landon and to watch him wrestle around in the floor with Ethan and Billy. No wonder their church is growing! He's just a big kid that sees the fun in everything. But above all that, I enjoyed watching you."

"What do you mean?" I questioned, not really sure I wanted to know the answer.

"I noticed that you wanted to make sure that everyone was happy. Yet, not really connected to anything that was going on."

"Guilty as charged!" I replied. "Social environments make me nervous. I haven't really been a social butterfly for the last twenty years."

"I know," Jenny said with a reassuring tone in her voice. "But I'm proud to see you coming out of your shell. I just want you to know that I love you and I am with you, supporting every step you take in that direction. What was your favorite part of Christmas, Chuck?"

"To be honest, I believe it was buying and handing out gifts to the nursing home. Partly because it took my eyes off of myself for a change, teaching me the valuable lesson that a lot of people were worse off than I've ever been. Even when I thought life was rough and unfair. And I have you to thank for that, Jenny. It was a great idea. It's something I want to do for the rest of my life. I hardly thought about Lizzie or Susie at all this Christmas. In fact, I feel a little guilty after the holidays were over, if you know what I mean?"

"Absolutely," Jenny replied. "It's fine to honor the past, Chuck, but it's unacceptable to live there. Life has too much to offer now to get stuck in our past."

As I listened to her talking about the past with passion while persisting to embrace the future, I wondered to myself if I should bring up that this was the anniversary of Rob's death. I decided against it since the whole purpose of the trip was to give her something else to think about. So I changed the subject.

"Jenny, do you have any idea why Shirley went to the doctor?"

"Yeah," Jenny explained. "She's been feeling drained lately. And she's had a persistent cough for over a month now. So she wanted to get a chest x-ray and a B12 shot. She thought they were both long overdue."

I chimed in in agreement. "I think she's struggling to keep up with a growing boy!" I declared, pointing with my thumb toward the backseat.

"How did your morning go with Max?" Jenny asked.

"I think it went really great. The more I get to know him, the more I respect and love him. Though I dare not say that out loud since Max is such a man's man!"

"That's funny!" Jenny said. "Max doesn't seem to struggle at all saying I love you. In fact, when we were at the ranch the other day, Billy told Blaze that he loved her and Max told Billy that Blaze loved him too and so did he!"

"Really! I'm shocked to hear that! I figured the only one that heard 'I love you' from Max would be Jesus and Peggy."

We both got tickled at that and began to laugh together. It sure feels good to do that! Laughter does my heart good.

"Getting back to your question, Jenny, I certainly feel like Max and I are getting closer each week. He certainly is filling a huge void left in my life by the death of Johnny."

"Ours as well," Jenny spoke up. "Billy really loves Max. He's like a substitute grandpa to him."

"That's a good way to put it. He has that homespun grandpa wisdom and I'm so thankful to have him in my life. He's helping me work through the maze in my past while navigating the plans of my future by teaching me to make wise decisions."

Four and a half hours seemed to pass in a few minutes as I saw the sign welcoming us to San Francisco. I announce it to the boys, summoning them to get on their shoes and hoodies. We easily found a parking place and headed for the entrance to AT&T Stadium. It was still well over an hour before game time. Thankfully we ordered our tickets online; I was glad we did because most of the crowd was standing in line to purchase them. We walked right through the gate.

Jenny took the boys with her. I have no idea where they were going but she left me a list of items to pick up at the concession stand. It looked more like a grocery list; I hoped I'd be able to carry it myself. I marveled at how much these two boys can eat. They single handedly polished off every single snack and soda that we brought with us. Yet it was apparent from the list in my hand that it had not affected their appetites!

I found our seats and started looking for them. It was almost thirty minutes before they showed up making their way down the aisle, with their faces painted blue and silver with wolves on each cheek. This was a first for me! Johnny and I would have never thought about this. I found myself a little jealous, silently wishing I had done it as well, whereby showing my true colors to the world.

The game got underway and it was a real clash! The pistol grip formation was more than Boston College had ever prepared for as we marched down the field uncontested time after time. The second half was different. They had figured out our game plan and began to pick away at our lead. The Wolf Pack, however, was triumphant by a score of 20-13 and boy, was I happy! I'd hate to think about the long drive home had we come out on the losing end.

It took us quite a while to get back on the road as 41,063 people rolled out of the stadium, some elated while others were deflated. This time we were on the winning side. Our star quarterback closed out his college career with over 9,900 yards passing and over 4,000 yards rushing. And we had a front row seat to watch history unfold.

Jenny was blown away by how the game started with the toss of a cookie, rather than a coin. It was an Oreo cookie, black on one side and white on the other. I guess you can say that we now know how the cookie crumbled!

It took us almost an hour to settle down once we got out of the city. We decided to eat supper before we made our way back home. I'll have to admit, as we were walking in to the restaurant, I was glad that we were on the winning side since Jenny and the boys were painted up like warriors on the warpath. It's just a lot more fun winning than it is losing!

Our conversation on the way home grew more interesting as we discussed our vision for the future. It was apparent that we loved each other deeply; after all, we aren't children. Our future is more about balancing our responsibilities and blending them together if we hoped to live in harmony. Our discussion covered a variety of subjects, from finances to family and on to more serious things as adoption, where we would live, etc. By the time I pulled into Jenny's house, at two o'clock in the morning, I felt like I was the one who had played in a football game. I was sore and stiff as I opened the door and stepped out into the brisk, night air.

Jenny woke the boys and helped them into the house and to bed. I unloaded the SUV in the meantime and stepped inside, waiting for her to come downstairs. I chuckled as she appeared at the top of the stairs; the light was reflecting on her face and you could still see the two little wolves on each of her cheeks. As we embraced at the bottom of the stairs, I said, "I love you, Jenny. Thanks for the fabulous day."

"No, thank you!" she whispered. "By the way, I haven't thought about Rob all day long. I kind of felt guilty when I saw his picture above Billy's bed. I do feel like we are putting our history in its proper place as we open the doorway to our future."

We kissed goodnight and I headed home. When I walked in the door, I saw my reflection in my mirror. I began to laugh; I had her paint all over my face.

I picked up my journal and sat down at the kitchen table. Opening to the next blank page, I wrote this title for today's entry: Finding Balance/Bringing Closure. What had I learned that is worth writing down?

- All of us have a history filled with past pain.

- It's OK to honor history but we can't live there.
- History can rob us of destiny.
- The key to a happy life is finding the balance between history and destiny.
- History contains our pain but destiny contains our possibilities.
- Balance always precedes progress.
- Don't close the history book until you've extracted the wisdom taught by experience.

Time to wash my face and hit the sack. I couldn't wait for church tomorrow. I've got a lot of things to praise Him for.

Chapter 9

Life is Filled with Surprises

I awoke with a sense of expectation. To be perfectly honest, I wondered all week what Max had been up to on the project. The day finally arrived to view his surprise. What he didn't know is that I have a surprise of my own and I'm equally anxious to witness his response.

Enough of that for the time being! I'd better get a move on. I'm meeting Max at nine o'clock at the shop, giving me a little over an hour to eat, shower, and do my devotion.

With my shower and breakfast behind me, I sat down with my devotional and opened it, revealing the title for today's rendering: The Secrets of the Samurai. This devotion was about the Samurai soldiers that lived in the twelfth century under Imperial Japan. These soldiers were a group of common servants. In fact, their name roughly translates as "those who serve." Yet this group were trained warriors who were skilled in the art of war. Their strategy was to infiltrate the society as servants and to battle from within the system to overthrow the dictatorship of the Shoguns and to bring freedom to their people. They were some of the first market-place ministers, so to speak, bringing change to society through servanthood.

The Samurai were armed supporters of wealthy landowners but they had one unique quality that was noteworthy. They never drew their swords unless it was to be used to draw blood. In other words, the secret to their victory was found in the surprise attack.

The writer likened our lives as Christians to the Samurai warrior. We, too, are called to serve God by serving others in the marketplace. We, too, must be skilled in handling the sword, "the Word of God," according to 2 Timothy 2:15. And we, too, must draw the sword of the Spirit from the sheath of our heart only to penetrate the works of darkness or evil.

It's amazing that the struggle of the Samurai went on for over two hundred years but they finally prevailed. The story ended with three simple words that were very profound: Never Give Up!

What an inspiring story to know that victory can be achieved with servanthood training and perseverance. If it worked for the Samurai, it can work for us today. The real key is keeping the main thing, the main thing and being persistent. We can't lose if we don't give up. Regardless of where we are in the process, we must keep on keeping on until we see the change that we desire.

Walking toward the truck I noticed a great contrast between the sharp winter wind and the sun shining brightly overhead, reminding me once again of what I once read. There's a new day before me as well as an opportunity to make a difference. I just pray that I am up to the challenges that it presents.

I was a little nervous as I pulled up to the shop. I felt like the prodigal son coming home to his father. Although I knew that somehow everything would turn out all right. With a shout, "Hello!" I announced my arrival. Max responded by inviting me to come on back.

I was shocked to find him sitting on the old wire spool. As he finished up his last swig of coffee, a sheepish grin creased across his face, and he asked, "Are you ready for your surprise?"

"Sure," I said, taking a seat on his work stool. Though I felt totally unworthy to be sitting on his perch!

Max reached up to the top shelf and pulled down a small box measuring about four by four. He removed the top and extracted something in a white, linen cloth. It disappeared in his big hands as he unwrapped it. There before me was a perfect circle with a beautiful cross in the middle. Yet on each side of the cross was compass points for north, south, east, and west. It looked amazing. He began to explain the pommel to me.

"The pommel is to bring balance to the sword, nothing I imagine can bring more balance to our lives than the cross of Jesus Christ. It is also from that very cross that we gain direction when we lose our way."

His words brought tears to my eyes. I responded, "That's perfect, Max. Absolutely perfect! It will stand on top of the sword as an external reminder that Jesus is in charge. I absolutely love it!"

I felt as if I were receiving a confirmation from God Himself as he placed the pommel in my hand. Suddenly I realized that God was indeed leading my life and was helping me to make sense of it all.

"I have a surprise to share with you also, Max."

"Really," he said with that smile that assured me that he already knew the surprise that was coming. He continued, "What might that surprise be?"

"Jenny and I are getting married!" I blurted out like a teenager.

"Is that right?" he responded. "Well, I must admit, I'm not really shocked! I kind of saw that coming for a while. When is the big day?"

"We want to make it a Valentine's Day wedding. Well, not exactly," I found myself stammering for the right words. "Valentine's weekend. Since Valentine's Day is on Monday, we are planning to get married on Saturday the twelfth so that we can spend all of that weekend at Lake Tahoe."

"Well! Sounds like you've got it all figured out. Have you bought the little lady a ring yet?"

"Nope. I plan to do that today, in fact. I know exactly which ring she wants. We went window shopping at Herzog's Jewelers when we were Christmas shopping at the mall. She dropped plenty enough hints to direct me to the right one!"

We both chuckled as he spoke up, "They have a way of doing that, you know!"

"Well, I can't say that I know, Max, but I sure am learning! I do have a bit of a problem though. The wedding is only a month away. And in three weeks, we have to have the sword done and present it to JD. We still don't have the scabbard made, nor the ring that attaches it to the belt of his uniform. And I must get ready for the wedding and make plans for the honeymoon…"

"Slow down!" he interrupted, "Before you work yourself up into a heart attack! I can finish the project from here. I am a silversmith, you remember. That will take part of the pressure off of you while you deal with the wedding stuff. I certainly don't want to get involved in the wedding planning!" He chuckled while removing the pommel from my hand and placing it back in the small box.

"I really don't want to be a part of the planning either," I said. "Seems like Jenny and Shirley are doing most of the planning and I'm just doing what I'm told."

"That's a good beginning for a happy home," he said with a smile. "Just do what you're told and you ought to get along well."

"Speaking of Shirley, she called me this morning and said she wanted to talk to me before I leave for Reno. I'm really not sure what she wants to talk about. She's been pretty sick here lately."

"Yeah, I know she has," Max said. "I heard them turn in a prayer request for her this morning."

"I guess I'd better get over there, Max, and check on her. I want you to know that you are a real life saver and I can't begin to tell you how much I appreciate you finishing the project!"

"Oh, that's what partners are for, you know, to cover one another, especially when one finds himself in a bind. You'd better run along and take care of your wedding plans. I don't want you to get in trouble this early in the process."

"Thanks again, Max," I said, and I left.

Driving toward Shirley's house, I couldn't help but think what a blessed man I was to have someone in my life like Max as a partner, as he calls it that would be willing to cover me in this hectic time.

Pulling down the driveway, I was a little surprised as everything seemed unusually quiet. I really expected JD to be buzzing around the farm on his four wheeler, but it was parked inside the garage. Sometimes I forget that teenage boys don't get up until noon!

Shirley responded to my knocking, "Come on in and grab you a seat. I'm in the kitchen."

I took my normal place at the table but something just didn't feel right this morning.

"Would you like a cup of coffee?" she asked.

"Sure," I said. "You know me; I never turn down a free cup of coffee, especially yours."

"Have you talked to Landon and Renee lately?" she inquired.

"No, not since the week after Christmas. Why? What's going on?" I asked as she sat the coffee in front of me.

"It's me, Chuck," she responded. "I talked to them about it last weekend when I was down to visit Jonathan and I thought they may have mentioned it to you."

"Not a word! Mentioned what?"

"I got my report back from the doctor and they discovered that I have lung cancer."

"Oh no, Shirley!" I said, raising to my feet and taking her in my arms.

She broke and began crying on my chest as I stood there with a million thoughts running through my mind. Yet no words seemed appropriate for the moment.

After a few minutes, I broke the silence and asked if JD knew.

"No. And I don't want him to know until after his Eagle Scout presentation. Promise me that you won't tell him."

"I won't, Shirley. I promise!" Her secret was safe with me. "What are the doctors saying?"

She swallowed hard and then replied, "They're saying I have six months to a year to live. And that's really what I want to talk to you about, Chuck, JD's future. He's at Jenny's right now. I asked her to come by and pick him up this morning so that we could really talk and figure out what we need to do."

"Shirley, I don't want you to worry a thing about JD. I promise you that he will never want for anything as long as he's alive. Neither will you! We are family. All I want you to focus on is getting better. Remember that God is still in control and nothing takes him by surprise."

"I know," she responded, taking a seat at the table across from me.

"I've already talked out a lot of the pain with Landon and Renee last weekend. They encouraged me to talk to Jonathan as well while I was there. I hated to do that so badly, especially since I was there to celebrate a belated Christmas with him. He took the news well or as good as could be expected. But once again, it caused him to battle with guilt. He feels like a total failure as he kept saying to me over and over, 'I would give my right arm to be there for you, Mom. Especially now. But I'm stuck in here for seven more years.' I tried my best to settle him down and assure him that God has everything under control. I went on to tell him how great you have been to JD and me since Johnny's death. And how well JD had adjusted. He told me to tell you thank you from the bottom of his heart."

"That's nice," I replied. "But seriously, that's just a drop in the bucket compared to what you guys have done for me. You've been part of my family for years. We've come through a lot together and we're going to fight through this as well. It's just what families do. They cover each other, especially when one finds himself in a bind." This recalled to my mind the statement that Max had said to me earlier. Little did I know I would need his nugget of wisdom so soon. "Is there anything we can do for you right now, Shirley?"

"Nothing but pray," she said. "And act normal so JD doesn't suspect anything. Honestly, I'm feeling OK at the moment. I just keep coughing. But I've convinced him that it is just part of winter. We'll cross the other bridges when we come to them. But for now, we've got an Eagle Scout presentation to attend and a wedding to plan. That's about all I can say grace over for the moment." She stood to her feet, closing the discussion for now.

We embraced, and I kissed her on the cheek and told her that I loved her. And I pledged to her that we were in it for the long haul. Though, I must admit, I identified with Jonathan as I made my way to the truck, leaving her in the doorway alone. I know in my heart of hearts that none of us are ever alone. He's always with us, on the mountaintop of victory and in the lowest valley of despair. He has promised that He will never leave us, nor forsake us, but to go with us always, even to the ends of the world.

I looked forward to the drive to Reno. There was much in my mind to process. In fact, it wasn't even noon and I felt like I'd been riding in an emotional roller coaster for days. Once again, I was reminded of just how precious life is, how we must learn to take advantage of every moment, and how foolish I have been to let my history rob me of my destiny.

My first thought was to run straight to Jenny's house, but that couldn't happen because JD was there. I toyed with the idea of returning to the shop to talk to Max, but deep inside of me, I knew what I should do. It was the time to run to Jesus and allow Him to direct my steps. I would remember this as a defining moment in my walk with the Lord. In fact, it was ironic that Pastor Jim just preached on Proverbs 3:5-6, "Trust in the Lord with all thine heart; and lean not unto thine own understanding. In all thy ways acknowledge him, and he shall direct thy paths." Now I found myself at a crossroads, called to walk this scripture out.

The more I rode, the more I cried, and prayed, and pondered, asking God to give me direction for the future. I can truly say that all I knew at the moment was the next step or two to take. It was God's will that I marry Jenny. And I also knew that He would have me adopt Billy, for they come as a packaged deal. Billy needed a father at this crucial time in his life, a real dad and not just a male role model. I intended to make it official. It was time for me to step up and take the responsibility as the spiritual leader of my family. I've run from reality long enough and I want to take the steps to do what's right. After all, that's all God requires from us: To pray and hear his voice and to obey Him by taking the next step in the journey. He is Lord, and we are His servants called to fulfill the Father's plan.

Once again, I feel waves of gratitude poured over me as I began to count the blessings of God in my life, praising Him for my job, my health, my relationships with Him, with Jenny, with Billy, with JD, Shirley, Landon, Renee, John, Rachel, my niece, my nephews, my church family, and on and on the list went as I kept praising him all the way to Reno and back home. A feeling of peace flooded over me. All I knew for sure was that God had everything in control. All along He had orchestrated my life for His purpose, placing the very people around me necessary to sustain me that I may reach my potential and bring glory to His name.

Spending the afternoon alone with the Lord resulted in a peace and assurance that I was not alone in the struggle. God is weaving a tapestry and each one of us is nothing more than a thread woven for His glory. He has created us for relationship and we must learn to love Him with all our hearts and to love and serve others. Only in doing so will we discover the fulfillment that servanthood can bring.

The lights of Fallon came into view. With the ring secure in my pocket and peace in my heart, I really was not willing for this moment to end. I felt as if I had delivered my very soul to the Lord and now He was carrying the burden that had been weighing me down. In the process, I had learned a valuable lesson: He truly desires to be our burden bearer and He alone fully understands what we are going through. 1 Peter 5:7 is true; we can cast our cares upon Him, knowing that He cares for us.

My supper came from the drive-thru at McDonalds. I still really wanted to see Jenny but I've decided it may be better to give her a call tonight instead.

I waited until I ate and cleaned up before retrieving the ring box from my coat pocket to have another peek. There it was, a perfectly cut one carat diamond solitaire, surrounded by another carat of baguette diamonds, with each facet reflecting light in its own special way. They had one thing in common, they were all birthed under pressure, selected and positioned by a master jeweler, and attached side by side for maximum effect. As the light danced in the facets, I realized how beautiful life can truly be when we find our place and simply shine.

Laying the ring box on the table, I picked up my journal, and turned to the next blank page, writing out this title: Life is Filled with Surprises. What have I learned today?

- Life is filled with unexpected moments.

- Not all surprises are good ones.
- God is never taken by surprise.
- God has a plan even in our difficult moments.
- God uses pressure to create beauty.
- Things only change for the better when we place them in God's hands.
- God always surrounds us with others to reflect His glory.

The roller coaster ride has ended, leaving me with a brand new perspective and a sense of courage to face life. There's really nothing to fear as long as we allow Him to ride along beside us.

I knew I'd better give my girl a call. I had a lot to process with her. First of all, I thanked Jesus for never leaving me alone.

Chapter 10

Between a Rock and a Hard Place

Emotions flooded me on this cold winter morning as the harsh Santa Ana winds blew through the valley. Maybe it was due to the fact that everything looked so dismal outside; not a sign of life anywhere to be found. Yet those of us who have experienced life know that things are not as dead as they appear. Winter is a season in the cycle of life where the sap has returned to the roots for the expansion of spring. This proves the point that what we see is temporal but the unseen is eternal.

I'm sure that part of my feelings was attached to Shirley's medical report. I can't imagine life without her. At the same time, I was excited and maybe even a little scared about what life will be like with Jenny and Billy and wondered if I'm up to the challenge before me. One thing was more than certain: I was more emotional than I'd been in decades.

Once comfortably seated at the table with my coffee nearby, I retrieved my devotional. Did it hold the answers for what I needed? It often did. As I opened it to my bookmark, I read the title greeting me: Between a Rock and a Hard Place. It is the story of Aron Ralston, a young engineer from Utah who enjoyed hiking in the Utah's Canyonlands National Park. On this particular day in question, everything seemed typical as he entered Blue John Canyon with everything he thought he would need for a day of hiking fun. It would become anything but typical!

The story described how he lost his footing and fell into a canyon slot, a boulder pinning his arm against the wall. He cried out in pain, but no one responded nor would they, as hours turned into days. He decided to use his video recorder to capture the entire event that would turn into one hundred twenty-seven hours.

The timing for this devotional was so interesting, for the movie had just come out the first week of November. Jenny and I even talked about going to see it, but we never got around to it. I guess it just wasn't the time. Apparently the time for me to learn more about this story was now.

The title alone describes my feelings perfectly. The story tells how he tried to chip at the boulder to no avail as he rationed his provisions for one day to nearly five. Somewhere in the process he decided that his only hope of survival was to amputate his own arm, using a dull utility tool to accomplish the task. He went into great detail, describing the excruciating pain and mental anguish he endured before he was finally free.

Once free, the ordeal was far from over. He would have to rappel down a 65-foot rock face with only one arm while the other was in a tourniquet made from the insulation from his camelback tube. He drove the nail in place and clipped on the rope that would guide him to safety. He described the fear he felt as everything he was and everything he hoped to be would hang on that single nail and ring. Fortunately, he found a pool of rain water that replenished his fluids and was eventually found by a family and helicoptered out by the Utah State Police to a medical facility close by where he was nurtured back to health.

When interviewed about the whole ordeal, he said that he had been able to reduce the process to two statements:

a. There's no force more powerful than the will to live; and,
b. Every second counts.

Tears rolled down my cheeks as I read these words. How true it is that God has given us the desire to live our lives to the fullest and to make every second count. The problem is our thoughts of the future often cloud out the present. And as in my case, we allow the pain from the past to prevent us from the potential of future happiness.

Nevertheless, it was time to get going. My first stop was to check with Max on the status of our project. The drive across town was frigid and the truck struggled in vain to get warm. I parked out front in my normal place and quickly made my way inside. The heat from the back welcomed me like a precious friend as I heard Max's deep voice shout out, "Chuck, is that you?"

"Yep," I responded.

"How are you, my friend?" Max questioned, as he stuck out his big hand to shake mine.

"I guess I'm OK," I grunted out and I took my place on the wire spool that I have dubbed my 'stool of learning.'

"Well, you don't seem that fine! You ain't getting cold feet are you?" Max said with that familiar grin.

"No, it's nothing like that," I assured him. "I just feel so torn in my emotions. On one hand, I'm excited about the potential of life with Jenny and Billy. On the other hand, I'm struggling with Shirley's health and how JD is going to handle the news. Or maybe even greater, how I'm going to handle JD! There are a lot more questions than answers in my life right now. I'm not even sure how I'm supposed to feel or not feel about the matter. What do you think?"

"Maybe that's the problem," Max replied. "You're relying on your feelings more than your faith. Feelings are constantly changing but God remains the same. God knew every bit of this long before you were born and He trusted you enough to put you right in the middle of it. The secret is, He hasn't called you to carry the burden, for He is our burden bearer! He is that nail in a sure place on which we can fully rely."

"Wow, Max! You amaze me by what you say," I interrupted. "I just read a devotion about a mountain climber named Aron Ralston that used that same term, a nail in a sure place! A nail that's so secure that you could hang your life and confidence on it. No doubt that nail is Jesus Christ."

"You're right, son," Max replied. "We get into trouble when we try to carry the yoke that is built for his shoulders."

"Thanks, Max, so much. You know exactly what to say. Or maybe even more, what I need to hear! I appreciate your help so much."

"Speaking of help," Max said, apparently feeling somewhat uncomfortable of the conversation, "let me show you how the scabbard turned out. I just finished it last night and put it up here on the top shelf for safe keeping."

With that, he reached up and pulled down the old box that had originally held the silver blanks before the project ever began. There inside was the sword, assembled and resting in the most beautiful scabbard that you could ever imagine. On the top was a replica of the Boy Scout Eagle patch with the wings of the eagle in full spread. Two words were on the banner that was carried in its talons: Be Prepared.

Underneath the patch was JD's name. The rest of the scabbard was decorated with a mixture of silver and gold, representing both strength and purity. It was simply magnificent.

"Max! This is perfect! Finally, our dream has become a reality."

"Well, I'm glad you like it. But in reality, I'm not finished yet."

"What do you mean?" I asked.

"There's one thing still lacking."

"What?" I inquired.

"The ring," he answered. "The ring attaches the sword to the soldier."

Suddenly I realized that the sword is useless without the ring. The ring is like our faith that connects us to the potential of God's ultimate power.

Max interrupted my thoughts by saying, "About the ring—I've got an idea."

"What's that?" I responded.

"I'd like to make three rings."

"Three rings? For what?"

"I'd like to make wedding bands for you and Jenny as my gift to you guys."

I know I probably shouldn't have, but my emotions got the best of me, and suddenly I found myself with my arms around Max's neck, hugging him and saying, "I'd be honored. Thanks so much!"

He cleared his throat and said, "You'd better get out of here for now so I can get to work." I'm almost sure I saw a tear in his eye before I made my way to the truck.

For some reason, I couldn't get Shirley off my mind, so I knew I should go and check on her. As I pulled down the driveway, nothing stirred but the wind. The trees swayed to its demand. I hurried inside, giving a shout to announce my arrival. Shirley responded back, "I'm in the kitchen."

"Aren't you always?" I said jokingly.

"It sure seems like it," she replied. "I can't seem to fill up this growing boy!"

"Where is JD?" I asked.

"He's upstairs taking a shower and packing up his clothes."

"Where's he going?" I quizzed.

"We're going down to see Jonathan this weekend. Since we're all going to be busy the next two weeks, I decided to go to Ely and surprisingly, he wanted to go with me. I think Jonathan will be so glad to see him. He was pretty broken when I left him the last time."

"I can only imagine what he must be feeling," I responded. "How are you feeling now, Shirley?"

"To be honest, I'm not doing so well. I'm physically tired, I'm physically drained. It's becoming more difficult to get my breath. In fact, I become winded with every little thing I do. But I must admit that the most aggravating thing is being forced to slow down my pace of life. I don't do so good at 'slow' if you know what I mean."

"Yep. I know exactly what you mean. I do feel like God is trying to make me slow down and get the best of every moment. That's not necessarily a bad thing, Shirley."

"I know," she responded. "Life is short at its longest and we should make every second count."

"Funny you should say that," I replied. "I just read the same statement in my devotion this morning. God must really be talking to me."

Suddenly I heard JD bounding down the steps. It sounded more like a freight train coming through the living room as he swung open the kitchen door. "Hey Uncle Chuck," he said as he gave me a high five and a hug.

"Well, Grandma, I'm packed up and ready to go."

"Where you headed?" I asked as if I were clueless of the answer.

"Grandma and I are headed down to see my dad. I haven't seen him in a while so I thought I would go this time. Besides I didn't want Grandma to drive down there by herself."

"Those are two good reasons for going," I responded as I put my hand on his shoulder. "I'm really proud to see you thinking of others and being so considerate. You're turning into a real gentleman! By the way, are you looking forward to your Eagle Scout ceremony next week?"

He kind of dropped his head toward the ground as he responded, "Yes and no. I'm excited to get my patch because I've really worked hard for it. But I so wish that Grandpa and Dad could be here to witness this day."

"Somehow I feel like that they might. Maybe not physically, but in their spirit. I know they are very proud of you, JD. We all are! Just think of it, you'll be tying the record for one of the youngest scouts to receive the Eagle award. That's quite an accomplishment and you deserve to be honored, young man!"

"Thanks, Uncle Chuck," he uttered, as a huge smile came across his face.

I continued, "Soon I'll be able to tell all my friends that I know an Eagle Scout personally!" He began to blush a little as I stoked the fire.

"Well, Grandma, I'm going up to get my suitcase."

"Grab mine as well," Shirley said. "It's at the foot of my bed. We'll get going as soon as I put these dishes away."

I realized that this was my cue so I said, "Well, I'd better get going so you guys can hit the road." With that I hugged her tightly and told her that I loved her. She didn't respond but I heard her sniffle. So I went on, "Tell Jonathan, 'Hello,' as well as Landon and

Renee." Once again I realized how thankful I am for all of God's blessings. To think that God would call my brother to pastor in the same town where Jonathan would soon be imprisoned. His blessings are just too many to count.

Shirley brushed a tear away from her eye with her apron as her voice began to break. She told me she loved me and wanted to thank me for making over JD like that. I assured her that everything was going to be OK and I encouraged her to enjoy her time with Jonathan and to make every second count.

I have to admit that I felt like I got back on that emotional roller coaster at full speed as I made my way toward the truck. Taking a glance at my watch, I realize that it's nearly two o'clock. This morning had flown by!

Jenny, Billy, and I had our first family night out scheduled at 5:30 PM and I already felt emotionally spent. A nap was definitely in order. Tonight was a very important occasion; our plan was to talk to Billy about adoption and I was a nervous wreck. Jenny has assured me over and over that he will be happy with the news. But I'm not that sure. One thing was certain and that is, I had to get a hold on my emotions.

When the clock went off at 4:45 PM, I hardly knew where I was. Dazed and confused, I felt like I had been in a coma instead of napping. I'm coming to discover that emotions can wring you out like a dishtowel and hang you out to dry. In a few minutes I felt a bit better, so I freshened up.

Billy had told me what clothes I needed to wear and said I should come in tennis shoes even though the weather demanded that I wear boots. Jenny and I decided to let him pick the restaurant and the activities for the evening and he assured us that he had everything under control.

As I pulled up to the house, I paused a moment and took a deep breath. I tried to imagine what this was going to feel like as a part of a daily routine. The thought made my heart begin to race. Jenny opened the door and I heard in the background Billy saying, "Do you think he will like it?"

"Like what?" I said, as I made my way inside.

Billy began to giggle as Jenny spoke up to cover him. "He was wanting to know if you would like the plans that he has made for tonight."

"I don't know. Let me hear them." I grabbed him in a bear hug.

"First of all, do you like pizza?" he asked.

"Absolutely! It's one of my favorites," I replied.

"Well, do you like bowling?"

"Yes, I love bowling. Why?"

"Then that settles it! We are going to Oasis Bowl and Family Fun Center for pizza."

I was a little taken back at first, and then it hit me. What a perfect place for our first family outing—the Family Fun Center!

"The perfect selection!" I said, as I slung him around in the air a few times before letting his feet touch the ground. Jenny was grinning from ear to ear. They donned their coats and we headed out the door for a family night of fun and pizza.

The place was packed and you could hardly hear yourself think. Quite a contrast from my normal lifestyle of eating alone and listening to myself chewing! One thing stood out about this place—it was filled with life and excitement as families were making memories and living life to the fullest, a trade that I was more than willing to make.

Billy hit the arcade games with a pocket full of tokens as Jenny and I ordered pizza and screamed out our conversation in a corner booth. I don't know when I had enjoyed myself so much. Just to see the smiles on Jenny and Billy's faces told the whole story. Tonight was shaping up to being a great success.

Jenny and I decided that we could not talk to Billy there; we would talk to him later. All the way home, he kept joking about what a lame bowler I was. I made him promise to give me a rematch and told him that things would surely be different the next time.

When we walked in the house, Billy hugged me and told me thanks for a great evening but I responded, "Sorry, buddy. I can't take the credit for this one. You're the man that made the plan for the evening and I want to thank you for letting me be a part!"

He smiled and responded, "You're more than welcome, sir!"

Suddenly the timing seemed right. "How about we close out our night with our first family meeting?" I proposed. "All in favor, say 'Aye'." We all voted yes as we made our way to the couch.

"Let me begin by calling this meeting to order. First on the agenda, we must select a name. I make a motion that we call this group, the Haynes Club. All in favor, say 'Aye'." Jenny and I both shouted out, "Aye" but Billy didn't know exactly what to do.

Finally, with an awkward smile, he said, "But my name is Sizemore. I know that when you and Mommy marry, her name will become Haynes but what about me?"

"That's exactly what this meeting is about! I want to adopt you Billy and give you my name. How would you like to become Billy Haynes?"

"I'd love to," Billy said. "Are you really wanting me to be your son?"

"Yes," I said as tears rolled down my face.

"That would be the greatest thing in the world," Billy said. "I won't have to explain to the kids at school that I don't have a dad anymore."

"Well the truth is, Billy, you have two dads. Your first dad died with great honor, defending our country and I, in no way, want to ever try to take his place. But I love you, son, and I want to be a dad to you for the rest of your life."

"But what will I call you, Uncle Chuck?"

"You can call me whatever you decide to. We can deal with that later. I just wanted to get your OK."

"Wow! This is the greatest day of my life," Billy said as we shared a group hug. "Mom's getting a new husband and I'm getting a new dad!"

And with that, we voted to adjourn the meeting. Billy went running toward the steps shouting out, "I'm going to go write this down in my journal." We could hear him mumbling to himself as he made his way up the steps, "Billy Haynes! Billy Haynes! Billy Haynes!"

There Jenny and I stood, arm in arm, with tears flowing, totally amazed at what we had just witnessed. It's true that you can never overestimate the power of just one moment and I never wanted this moment to end! But it was getting late and I needed to leave. I could feel our tears co-mingling as I held her face close to mine, hugging her tightly. After a few moments, I pulled out my handkerchief, dried away her tears, kissed her on the forehead I told her, "Well, I guess we are a family now."

She walked me to the truck, we kissed goodnight, and I headed home. What a climactic end to a roller coaster day! Things could not have gone better. I am one blessed man.

As I walked into my house, I picked up my journal, and turning to the next empty page, I inscribed the title, Between a Rock and a Hard Place. What did I learn today?

- Life has seasons, some of sorrow, some of joy.
- Winter to one may be spring to another.
- Cherish every moment, good or bad.
- Make every second count.
- Take time to slow down and celebrate.
- Face your fears with faith.
- Always keep a grateful heart.

Reflecting over the day's events, I came to realize that this had been a full day. I laughed, I cried, I loved, but above all, I made every second count. "Lord, please help me to do the same thing tomorrow. Amen!"

Chapter 11

Alone Yet Not Alone

The big day of celebration arrived. JD would receive his Eagle Scout award. This is quite a milestone in his life as he will be tying the record as the youngest recipient of this great honor. I can't help but think of the countless hours that Johnny spent with him in preparation for this special day. It seemed almost unfair that he would not be there to witness it. But once again I'm reminded of just how many lives he affected and how all of us have the opportunity to invest in others if we are willing to take it. Life is filled with twists and turns and the secret to success is to make deposits in the lives of those we meet along the way. It's more about the journey than it is the destination.

My devotion would be just the thing to start this exciting day. We're all scheduled to meet for a luncheon at eleven o'clock at the Fallon Convention Center. There will be dignitaries from all over Nevada connected with the Boy Scouts of America organization. We will have representatives there from our regional offices in Reno, as well as the Director and Scoutmaster over the state. Following the event, Max has invited all of us to Circle K ranch for a BBQ and an afternoon of fun and games. I usually shy away from social events, but I wouldn't miss this presentation for all the money in the world. It isn't just a presentation of an award but a milestone in the life of a young boy as he embraces manhood. I know the transitions in life are never easy, but they're necessary for our development.

As I open my devotional, I see a bold title with four words:

Alone Yet Not Alone. It is the story of Joni Eareckson Tada born October 15, 1949 in Baltimore, Maryland, the youngest of four daughters who grew up to be quite a tomboy. As a teenager, Joni enjoyed a variety of hobbies, including horseback riding, hiking, tennis, swimming, etc. But on July 30, 1967, everything would change as she went for a swim in Chesapeake Bay. Diving in the water, she suddenly realized she had misjudged its depth, striking the bottom in full force, crushing her neck between the fourth and fifth cervical levels, leaving her paralyzed from the shoulders down.

She recounts her frustrations that she experienced along the way and the plethora of emotions from anger to depression to suicidal thoughts, and even the doubts that attacked her religious faith. But after years of struggle, she came to realize that though her situation carried some characteristics that were unique and personal, she was not alone. Nor had she ever been.

One day she picked up a paint brush between her teeth and began to paint, uncovering a talent that she never knew existed deep inside her. As her talent began to grow, so did her acclaim, providing her the opportunity to explore her other interests. To date, she has authored more than forty books, recorded several music projects, starred in her own autobiographical movie, is a gifted speaker in great demand, as well as a known advocate for people with disabilities—all because she refused to lay down and quit. Wow! What a story of inspiration.

No matter how bad we think we have it, there's always someone who has it worse. How true it is that success is not determined by what happens to us but rather by what happens in us when we face difficult moments. Hardship has the ability to make us bitter or better; the outcome is up to us.

Time to get going. I had to meet Max at the shop at nine o'clock to pick up the sword. I tried to get him to bring it, but he refused and insisted that I need to pick it up and take it myself. One thing I've learned over the past several months, it's futile to argue with Max.

Stepping outside, I was greeted with a pleasant surprise—the weather was unusually warm for February fifth. The temperature gauge on the garage wall read fifty-five degrees. The high for the day was supposed to reach the low-to mid-sixties. Looks like a perfect day in every way!

Pulling up to the shop, I noticed immediately that Max's truck was parked in the front instead of its usual place. As I walked through the door, there sat Max behind the counter in Peggy's chair. I must admit, he looked totally out of place, sitting among all those silver trinkets and knick-knacks adorning the gift shop, though nearly all of them were products of his rough hands. The bigger shock however was how he was dressed. He wore a suit, or maybe I should say, Max's version of a suit. Dress jeans, cowboy boots, a white shirt, grey and black tweed sports coat with a bolo tie, topped off with a black velvet cowboy hat.

"Good morning, Max," I said, as he nodded his head and grunted out, "Morning."

"How are you feeling, and are you ready for today's presentation?" I asked.

"As ready as I will ever be," he retorted. "At least the sword is ready. For that I'm thankful. Have you talked to JD lately?"

"Yep! I've talked to him several times in the last week," I responded. "But he's still clueless about the sword. It's going to be a real surprise. Speaking of surprises, I wanted to ask a favor of you."

"What's that?" Max asked with a noticeable hesitation in his voice as he picked up the sword for one final examination.

"I want you to join me on stage for the presentation."

"I'm not sure I signed up for that one!" he blurted out.

I quickly responded, "I know, I know. But I talked to JD this week and his only regret was the fact that Johnny and Jonathan would not be there to witness his presentation and I kind of promised him that their places would not be vacant. I can only stand in for one and I don't know anyone better than you to stand in for the other."

"Well, since you put it that way," he said, "I guess I can't turn you down. But you are going to have to do all the talking."

"It's a deal!" I said, sticking out my hand to shake on it. "Shirley is actually going to do the presentation of the sword to JD after he receives his patch and certificate."

"OK," Max muttered. "Just remember, you have to do all the talking."

"I will," I replied, as I picked up the sword from the counter and headed toward the door.

"I'll see you there," Max called, and he threw up his hand in reply.

At home, I laid the sword and scabbard on the table, still amazed that it was finally complete and totally shocked at the finished product. It looked nothing like the original plan. It had taken on a life of its own through the process, with every alteration adding uniqueness and value. I guess you could say that it bore the marks of the process. The truth of the matter is that life leaves its mark on all of us.

When the time came for me to put on my monkey suit, I sighed. I was definitely a lot more comfortable in Wranglers and boots than I was with a coat and tie but sometimes you just have to take one for the team.

Jenny, Billy, and I are riding together to the Convention Center, but as I walk up to the door to get them, I felt like a fish out of water. I paused for a moment to check out my reflection in the window. I make a few needed adjustments to my tie but at the same time, she opened the door, catching me primping. Heat rose up my cheeks as she said with a wink, "I think you look just perfect!"

"Me?" I responded. "You look absolutely stunning!"

Her blond hair and blue-green eyes stood out against the navy blue dress and white jacket trimmed in navy. The pearl earrings and necklace completed her ensemble.

"I'm not sure I look good enough to sit with the likes of you," I said, leaning over to greet her with a kiss. "Where's Billy?"

"He's upstairs," she responded, "reluctantly taking a bath and putting on his uniform. I don't know what it is about young boys. The only thing they hate worse than social gatherings is taking a bath." Her statement caused us both to chuckle.

"How is he feeling about JD's big day? I certainly don't want him to feel lost in the shuffle."

"Actually, he's happy for him. We talked about it this morning. To be honest, he's still riding on cloud nine from our first family meeting. He continues to refer to himself as Billy Haynes. Though I warned him that it was a family secret and that all family meetings required secrecy."

"That's good," I said as Billy appeared at the top of the steps.

"Hey, Uncle Chuck…...I mean Chuck…...I mean Dad. Sorry," he said with a puzzled look on his face. "I'm not quite used to all of this quite yet."

"No problem," I reassured him. "It will all become natural over time. It's just a part of the process." I smiled as I quoted from my devotion this morning, though I wasn't confident in my qualification to speak the message yet since I'm still in the throes of change. "Are you excited about today's events?" I questioned.

"I'm excited about going to the ranch to see Blaze. Max told me that JD and I could ride his horses and JD wants to bring his four-wheeler today. It's going to be a blast!"

"Well, we'd better get going to the luncheon. It starts at eleven o'clock sharp and I'm sure the parking lot is already packed."

"Speaking of parking," Jenny interrupted. "Let's take the SUV. I'm really not for sure this is a pick-up truck event."

"Is that right!" I said as I winked to Billy in response. "You know us boys had better stick together. She's going to make sissies out of both of us yet."

I retrieved the sword from the truck and put it in the back seat with Billy for safekeeping. When I got into the car, I asked him if he would like to go for his Eagle Scout badge someday.

"I'd like to," he responded. "But I'm a long way from it since I got into the program a lot later than JD."

"I totally understand," I responded assuring him that I was not comparing him to JD. "I was just thinking that JD and I could help you reach your goal if you so desired. Everyone needs help from others some time in their life and I want you to know that I am here if you need me." That statement brought a smile both to his and Jenny's faces.

As expected, we had to park a good piece from the front door. Billy was our pace setter and Jenny and I walked behind him hand in hand. I left the sword locked in the car for safekeeping. I could run back and get it when the troop is called behind the stage prior to the ceremony.

We spotted our table as we entered the banquet hall. We were seated in the place of honor right in front of the stage. There at the table were Max and Peggy, Shirley and JD, with three empty places for Jenny, Billy, and myself. I thought to myself as I took my seat, "I'm surrounded by six people that had become family to me, reminding me of the truth I read this morning: Even though we think we are alone, we're never really alone." Of course, Jesus has promised to never leave us nor forsake us and as Christians we are constantly aware of that. But sometimes we forget that He has also surrounded us with wonderful treasures waiting to be mined and I'm so grateful for the table of treasures before me.

The meeting was called to order with the Pledge of Allegiance, the Boy Scout oath, and the invocation which included grace for the meal that was about to be served. When I opened my eyes, I noticed Max with his cowboy hat in his left hand and his right hand over his heart. I thought to myself, "What a wonderful example for these two young boys to witness." For Max has known the cost of war and the value of freedom, something that this next generation will have to learn.

We ate a wonderful catered meal as our conversation revolved mostly toward JD, which is exactly what it should have been. JD followed almost every statement, thanking us all for being there to celebrate with him until Max spoke up, easing JD's anxiety, with this statement, "Let me tell you something, young man. What you have accomplished is no small thing. Most people never reach this milestone until they are grown men. But your hard work and diligence has brought you here at only thirteen years of age. We all want you to know that we love you and that we are proud to sit at the table with you and with Billy, great scouts and even better, perfect young gentlemen. So congratulations!" And with that, the entire table applauded. Others around us may not have understood exactly what was going on at our table but it didn't seem to matter. For Max had summarized what everyone at the table was feeling. I grinned at myself as I recalled his words, "You need to do all the talking!"

Yeah, right, I thought to myself. You can say more in one minute than I can say in an hour and you always say it at just the right time.

As I looked around the table, my mind began to wander. I thought of how each of us had our gifts and our talents, but it was actually our voids and vacancies that had brought us together. Max and Peggy had lived a successful life, but yet they had no children or grandchildren to share it with. Shirley had a son and grandson, yet she lacked the family fellowship that life was supposed to bring. Jenny and Billy are hundreds of miles away from their family and need love and protection. JD needed the affirmation of a father and grandfather. And of course, my needs are too numerous to mention. To think it's not our strengths and talents that God uses but through His infinite wisdom, He strengthens us in our weakness that can far exceed the wealth of our gifts.

At that moment the emcee stepped to the microphone and announced that in five minutes, he wanted to meet with all the boy scouts on the stage to prepare for the presentations. For the rest of the ceremony, they would be seated on the stage with the rest of the dignitaries while the families, one by one, would join their scout onstage for the presentation of their badges. This would be my cue to grab the sword and place it by Shirley under the tablecloth to keep our surprise intact.

Everything went off as planned as the emcee returned to the podium, asking everyone to stand and to remain standing until after the National Anthem. As the boy scouts marched in, led by the dignitaries to their proper position, the Anthem began to play. You could feel the electricity in the air as the words were being mimed by everyone in the crowd. At the end of the Anthem, the room was filled with the cheers of patriotism as our hearts swelled with pride. The emcee lifted both hands to call the meeting back to order, encouraging us to take our seats, as he introduced the regional director of the Boy Scouts of America, stationed in Reno.

He began his remarks by honoring those seated on the platform with him and welcoming all the family members that had come to be a part of this celebration. But suddenly, his voice began to crack as he struggled to hold his emotions in check. "No man is an island," he said. "And no one ever rises to a position of power alone. I stand here before you today because of my dear friend and mentor, Johnny Dale. His impact into my life personally and to the Boy Scouts across this state cannot be measured. Before I proceed any further, we would like to take this opportunity to honor this great man and powerful leader with this brief video."

The lights dimmed and the face of Johnny Dale appeared on the screen, followed by an assortment of slides honoring his service. Among them were pictures of Jonathan, JD, and Shirley, from their former days as family, as Lee Greenwood's song "I'm Proud to Be an American" played softly in the background. There was not a dry eye in the place, mine included. My heart was overwhelmed to think how God has graciously granted JD's wish, allowing Johnny and Jonathan to make their appearance at his celebration. At the end of the video, the regional director asked JD and Shirley to stand. The people began to clap and stand to their feet all over the building. It is a moment I will never forget.

Once again, he asked us to take our seats and continued his remarks on the subject of teamwork. At his conclusion, he introduced the Nevada State Director to make the presentations. One after another, the scouts were called to the podium to be joined by their families to receive their badges and certificates until the climactic moment finally arrived when his name rang out: Jonathan Dale III.

At that moment we all stood and made our way to the platform with Max, Peggy, Jenny, and I shielding Billy and Shirley, carrying the sword. The director pinned the Eagle Scout badge on JD's uniform as he talked about how impressed he was with JD's accomplishment at such a young age. Upon the presentation of his certificate, JD received a standing ovation and his smile was beaming from ear to ear.

The director went on to explain, "I understand that the family has a presentation they would like to make as well." That was my cue to step forward and take the mike. To my surprise and gratitude, Max stepped up beside me to offer the moral support that I so desperately needed.

I began my remarks by saying, "I hardly know where to begin. This family means much more to me than words could ever express. For I, too, am one of the many lives shaped by Johnny Dale for over twenty years. I recall as if it were only yesterday the day that JD was born. I remember his first day as a Tiger Cub and I've been a first-hand witness of his journey through the various levels of the Boy Scouts. Over a year ago, Johnny called, wanting me to meet him for breakfast. He told me he had a proposal that he wanted to offer me. I had no idea what it was. He later explained that he wanted me to be a part of a project for a special gift to present to JD for this very day. Unfortunately, Johnny was taken away from us a few months ago. However, God has so graciously brought another mentor and father figure into my life, Max Hammon, who stands here beside me today. He has helped me to finish the project and make Johnny's dream come true. At this time, I would like for Shirley Dale, Johnny's wife, to present this special gift to JD."

Jenny, Peggy, and Billy all stepped aside as Shirley made her way across the stage while the light, reflecting from the sword, began to dance in JD's eyes. His mouth fell open in utter shock as the expression on his face silently asked the question, "Is this really for me?"

Suddenly, like a ton of bricks, it hit him that this was not just a sword but the dream of his grandpa, Johnny Dale, reaching back from beyond the grave to memorialize this moment. With trembling hands, he took the sword from Shirley. But the gravity of the moment was much too heavy for his young shoulders to carry as he crumbled into Shirley's arms and began to weep uncontrollably. There they stood together, center stage, facing the stark reality that manhood was calling him out of boyhood and they had no choice but to answer the call. JD would have to step forward and assume responsibility and Shirley would have to step back and release the child that she had cradled in her arms. It was then we all realized that we were witnessing a moment of transition while a memory was being formed that time could not destroy.

Pictures followed to seal this moment in time as JD and Billy went over every inch of the sword. Max finally got the opportunity to attach the sword to JD's belt as once again he described the importance of the connection of the soldier and his sword. Max reminded JD that this was not a toy, but a weapon used by men to defend and protect their families and that this weapon must be respected and handled with dignity. The sword nearly touched the ground but Max and I both knew for certain that he would grow into it over time. But for now, it was our duty to celebrate a milestone and celebrate we would!

We split up as we left the celebration to change our clothes with a promise that we would meet at Max and Peggy's ranch within the hour. Jenny and I took JD with us and told Shirley that we would stop by the house and pick up his four-wheeler and helmets so that the boys could ride. With every detail sorted out, we went our way.

Finally, everyone gathered together at the ranch to party. The girls gathered on the patio to talk and prepare the meal while the boys rode the horses around the corral. Max and I found ourselves leaned against the fence with our feet on the first rail as a gentle breeze blew in our faces.

"Well, what do you think about today, Max?" I said, breaking the silence.

Max paused for a moment, then replied, "I think maybe you and I just got the chance to be a part of something way above our heads. Whoever would have thought that two old cowboys like us would get the opportunity to address a crowd of distinguished leaders as we did today?"

"Yeah! Whoever would have thought it indeed?" I concurred as we both chuckled together.

We laughed, we played, we talked, and we ate until the afternoon turned into evening. It was obvious on Shirley's face that she was growing weary and it was time for all of us to say our good-byes. We hugged each other and headed home.

As I walked inside my house, my eyes were drawn to the three books that had become such a part of my everyday life: my Bible, my devotional, and my journal. Picking up the journal from the table, I sat down and began to write these four words across the top: Alone Yet Not Alone. It was now the time for me to condense this unbelievable day into a few lessons that I had learned.

- We are never really alone no matter how we feel.
- God's plan includes our strengths and our weaknesses.
- What's missing in one can be found in another.
- All of us are just pieces in God's great puzzle.
- We should never do life alone.
- Remember that life is a journey, not an event.
- Always take time to celebrate every milestone.

This day may very well stand out as the greatest day of my life. Though this day was not about me at all. It's funny but I've discovered that the greatest joy we can have in this life is making others' dreams come true. I've decided that this is what I want to do with the rest of my life. I prayed: "I want to thank you, Lord, for never leaving me alone even in my loneliest hour and for teaching me the joy of investing in others as we follow Your example of finding a need and filling it. There are dreams all around us and I, for one, am going to take my share. Thank you, Lord, I love you! Good night!"

Chapter 12

One Look Back Could Change Your Legacy

February 12, 2011. "My wedding day has arrived." That's the first thought in my mind as my eyes opened. The dim light in my bedroom substantiated the evidence that my plan to sleep in late this morning had not materialized. A glance at the clock revealed that it was only 6:16 AM. I got up and slipped on some clothes as I made my way quietly to the kitchen trying desperately not to wake up everyone in the house for I am not alone this morning. Everyone has come in for our wedding.

John, Rachel, Ellen, and Ethan were staying with me. Landon and Renee were at Shirley's. Their boys would drive up from Ely to be ushers in their "favorite uncle's" wedding. Jenny's parents were naturally with her. They came up Wednesday and would be keeping Billy until we return from our honeymoon.

Jenny and I would spend this morning with our respective families. Our wedding would begin at two o'clock and of course, everyone insisted that I cannot see Jenny until then. You know how those superstitions go!

Landon, Renee, Shirley, JD, John, Rachel, Ellen, Ethan, and I would meet at Jerry's Restaurant at eleven o'clock for brunch. Until then, we are all on our own.

I turned on the light over the stove, trying not to make a peep but you should know me by now, I have to have my coffee the first thing in the morning. Fortunately, my old coffee pot doesn't make a lot of noise so maybe I'd pull it off.

With my coffee in hand, I took a seat at the kitchen table. My mind was flooded with thoughts about my first wedding day. It was hard for me to believe that it was nearly twenty-five years ago. We were just kids, though we thought we were grown and ready to face life together. We had a perfect blend of ignorance and innocence, a perfect combination to jump-start a marriage. Everything was an adventure, a mountain to climb and a battle to conquer, but in reality we had no idea of what was really coming. All we knew was that we loved each other and that seemed to be enough for the moment. At best, it was a blind leap of faith, motivated by love, as we stood before a justice of the peace with my mom and dad as our only two witnesses. That certainly would not be the case today!

Jenny and I have talked countless hours over that past few weeks about everything you could imagine from finances to housing, to time management, to the adoption of Billy. You name it; it's been discussed, prayed over, and planned. Our decision to do life together was not a blind leap of two crazy kids. We are well aware that this decision involves the lives and future of other people. Therefore, we have sought God's approval and the counsel of people we trust. We realize that we do not have the time to recover as we did when we were children; we can't afford to make a mistake at this time in our lives.

I suppose I will take full advantage of my quiet time today to read my devotion. Today's offering has already perked my interest with the title alone that seems to be a paradox: One Look Back Could Change Your Legacy! The story is about Alfred Nobel, a name recognizable all around the world because of his connection to the Nobel Peace Prize, which has been given out for over a century to those that have excelled in the fields of Physics, Chemistry, Literature, Medicine, and those that have furthered the cause of peace. But that was not always the case.

Alfred Nobel was born October 21, 1833 in Stockholm, Sweden, the fourth child of eight children born to Immanuel and Caroline Nobel. He was a sickly child who was often confined to bed, leaving him alone with only his thoughts and imaginations to occupy his time. That, however, produced a mind filled with curiosity and wonder concerning the possibilities of life. A curiosity so great that common education could not quench. He would become fluent in five different languages: English, French, German, Russian, and of course, his native tongue, Swedish.

His father moved the family to Russia when Alfred was only four years old and began a factory manufacturing explosives. The success of the company soon afforded Alfred with the best of tutors under which he mastered Chemistry, opening the door for Alfred to travel the world at eighteen years of age. His travels took him to Paris, London, and the United States before he would return to Russia to join his father in the family business.

By now, Russia was involved in the Crimean War and Alfred was doing research to develop explosives and ammunition that would aid his country in warfare. After the war, his father's company declared bankruptcy and his family returned to Sweden. But Alfred continued his research, leading him to discover dynamite.

In 1888, Alfred's brother, Ludwig died in Paris. A French newspaper mistakenly reported the death of Alfred instead. The obituary included an editorial comment that Alfred's only major contribution to life was the invention of dynamite, the most destructive, deadly force known to man.

As Alfred read his own obituary, he decided to invest the bulk of his wealth, 250 million dollars by American standards to establish the Nobel Peace Prize. He said, "I refuse to be known as a man of death and destruction. I will be known as a man of peace!"

What a powerful story! It forced me to wonder about my own future. What will I be known for and what will be my legacy?

Laying down my devotional, I picked up my journal and began reading over the last few months of my journey. I realized that this is the only written document of my life. Everything else is contained in my memory. I knew my schedule will not allow me to carry out my normal routine so if I wanted to have a journal entry recorded, now was the time. It was appropriate, as I wanted a record of my feelings in this moment, as I stand poised between my past and my future.

With pen in hand, I write out the title: One Look Back Could Change Your Legacy. As I began to process the last twenty years, I decide to list these lessons from my life:

- Your past does not determine your future.
- Failures are never final.
- You can turn stumbling blocks into stepping stones.
- One great decision can change the rest of your life.
- You shouldn't allow your mistakes to define you.
- God is a redeemer of broken dreams.
- As long as there is life, there is hope.

As I closed my journal, I looked up to see Rachel walking into the kitchen. "You're up early," she whispered. "Are you feeling OK?"

"I'm fine physically," I responded. "But concerning my feelings, I've been sorting them out for the past hour or so." As I smiled and continued, "I've got a lot of mixed feelings this morning but deep inside, there's a settled peace I know I'm doing the right thing."

"I think so too," she responded, pouring herself a cup of coffee and taking a seat at the table. Finally, we could talk as adults without her feeling the need to rescue me from my past.

Over the next hour we talked uninterrupted about our childhood memories, our lessons from life, our pain, and even our children. It felt so good to not be the subject of conversation but rather, a participant. I realize that a few quality decisions that I had made over the last few months had changed our relationship drastically, removing the obstacles that had blocked our growth. Somehow I wished I had done this years ago but I've come to discover that wishing doesn't change anything and I refuse to live another second in my past.

Conversation continued, even as we joined the others at Jerry's Restaurant. We talked and laughed together as we rehearsed all of the events from the night before. Our wedding rehearsal was more like an unrehearsed Christmas play as Shirley tried, to no avail, to get us all to be serious. There was just too much nervous energy for any of us to stay focused. I was more than sure, however, it would all come together when the church is full of onlookers.

Landon and Pastor Jim would officiate our wedding. Max was slated to be my best man; JD, my groomsman. Rachel would stand by Jenny as her maid of honor and Ellen was a bridesmaid. I asked Shirley to join Jenny's mom in lighting the candles that we will use to light the unity candle. She is the closest thing I've had over the last decade to a real mom. And of course, Jenny, has asked Billy to walk her down the aisle this time.

Her dad was a little disappointed with her decision but reluctantly agreed when he saw how excited Billy was about it. Everything was settled but my nerves and hopefully they would join me somewhere in the process.

We sat around the table and talked the morning away but it was time to get ready. For some reason or another, Shirley and Jenny have demanded that we all be there for pictures. I don't know why it takes an hour to take a few pictures but I was not asked my opinion so apparently, it was not needed. I'll just do what I have been told.

We arrived at the church at one o'clock, and the first thing I saw were my two nephews, Russell and Robert, manning the door in their penguin suits. As I got out of my car, they called out in unison, "The old man has finally arrived!"

"I'll make you think 'old man.' I can still take both of you to the ground!" I said as I walked up the sidewalk.

They laughed and responded, "You'd better save your energy; you may need it later!"

We hugged each other and talked for just a second at the door. It was so good to see them again. I told them how honored I was that they would drive all the way from Ely to serve as ushers in my wedding.

Robert responded by saying, "We're just glad you got married before you got too old to travel!" They both laughed together. There's nothing they both enjoy more than grilling me.

Russell stepped inside to see if the way was clear for me to come in. Shirley had informed them that I could not come in before Jenny was out of sight. Shirley was in the vestibule as I walked in the church. She had been walking around like a chicken with her head cut off. She looked so pretty and happy, carrying out the duties that Jenny had assigned. She hugged me and kissed me on the cheek and then promptly marched me to the pastor's office as if I were in trouble, telling me to stay put until she returned.

As I opened the door, there stood Landon, Max, and JD with Pastor Jim sitting at his desk. They, too, were all waiting on Shirley's next instruction. We greeted one another and then Landon piped up with a question, "Are you nervous, baby brother?"

"Slightly," I responded. "Are you?"

"No, Pastor Jim and I do this all the time! We're not nervous at all. It's your life that is going to drastically change; we're just tying the knot."

They shared a great big laugh at my expense, but were quickly snapped to attention as Shirley entered with a tray of boutonnieres. She worked her way up from JD to Max, pinning them on each of us and making sure they all looked perfect for our presentation. I could hardly keep a straight face as she worked on Max's lapel. He looked about as comfortable as if she were pinning him with a rattlesnake. She then told us to follow her; it was time for pictures, as she tried to convince us that this would save a lot of time later.

We all nodded and followed along like a group of puppies as the photographer took every kind of picture you could imagine. Then Shirley ordered us back to the office to wait until our cue with the music.

It seemed to me like we were in there for a week and with every second, I grew more nervous. All of them did their best to make the moment light-hearted but I could still hear the crowd gathering in the auditorium. Finally, I heard the music begin to play as I watched through a crack in the door. Robert and Russell ushered in Shirley and Peggy and then Jenny's mom and dad to their respective places.

Once everyone was in place, they ushered up the moms to light the candles, calling the ceremony to order. That was our cue, as Landon and Pastor Jim led me, Max, and JD to the platform.

As the music continued to play, seamlessly the double doors opened and down the aisle came Ellen, wearing a beautiful red gown. I then realized why we were all wearing red carnations on our lapels. I thought it was because it looked good with our black tuxes but again I had been proven wrong.

Rachel followed and took her position, just to the right of Landon. As the double doors closed and the music softly ended, the wedding march began to play. Pastor Jim motioned with his hands for the congregation to stand.

Once again, the doors opened, there stood Billy and Jenny. Billy looked like a little man in his tux and Jenny looked radiant in an ivory colored gown. Her eyes were sparkling in the candlelight as she carried a bouquet of red roses in her hands. She looked like an angel to me as she made her way down the aisle to the front of the church.

Pastor Jim once again motioned for the crowd to be seated. Landon began the ceremony, "Dearly beloved, we are gathered here today in the sight of God and this company to join together this man and this woman in holy matrimony. Who giveth this woman to be wed?"

Billy responded loudly, "I do," as he reached up and gave Jenny a kiss on the cheek. She embraced him as you could hear every woman in the crowd sniffle. He then took his seat by his grandpa, receiving a hug of affirmation for a job well done.

As I took Jenny by the hand, we stepped in front of Landon and Pastor Jim. Landon could tell that I was a nervous wreck so he couldn't resist lightening the moment with, "Are you sure you want to do this, baby brother?"

Everyone laughed as I responded, "You bet, I am!"

He went on to explain the covenant that we were entering into before God. He then had us to repeat our vows one to another. Pastor Jim then stepped forward for the exchanging of the rings. He talked about the love that had been poured in to this gold and that Max had prepared these rings for this special occasion.

"From This Moment" began to play as we walked down together, lighting the unity candle in the middle and blowing out our two single candles as Pastor Jim led us in communion together.

We returned to the middle of the platform as Pastor Jim and Landon asked the congregation to join us as they both blessed our union. Then Landon told me that I could kiss my bride. This kiss was different than any kiss before. It was not the coming together of our lips but rather, the coming together of our lives.

Following was the announcement from Pastor Jim, "May I present to you: Mr. and Mrs. Chuck Haynes."

We made our way over to the reception hall where Renee had everything in place. It was simply gorgeous. And so was the wedding cake that she had made herself. Not only is she a wonderful cook, but she runs a little bakery in Ely where she specializes in cake decorating. It was her special gift to us. And of course, it was white, adorned with red roses. It was perfect!

We received the people, cut the cake, took more pictures, and enjoyed the moment. But to our surprise, it was interrupted by the sound of a fork clinging against a glass. As I looked around, there stood Max and with his rough, stern voice, he shouted, "May I have your attention, please!" You could have heard a pin drop.

"Well, I reckon it's my job to offer a toast," he declared. "Let me begin by saying—it took God and half the people in this room to get these two married off." Everyone broke into laughter as a big grin came across Max's face and he continued, "It'll take every one of us and Jenny to train Chuck in how to be a husband and father!" The laughter continued.

Max then paused for a moment and said, "Let me get serious here. These are two of the finest people I know in the whole wide world. And God has called them to raise up one of the finest little fellows I have ever met. And they're gonna do it because they've already realized that the secret to a happy home is to make Jesus Christ the Lord and Chief Architect! Would you join me in toasting their new beginning?"

People came to us one by one to congratulate and confirm our union but finally it came time for us to change our clothes and head to Lake Tahoe. Everyone gathered outside to throw birdseed and to wish us well.

As we made our way to the crowd, we noticed Billy and JD standing at the door. We stopped for a moment to give them a hug and then made our way on to the car, which, by the way, had been decorated to the hilt, thanks to my brother-in-law, John Wallace.

Driving away, I couldn't resist taking one last look in the rear view mirror at all the people gathered in the street that love us, believe in us, and are depending on us to lead the way. With Jenny's hand tightly in mine, I looked out the windshield at the road that lay before us. One thought permeated my mind, and I knew it would be one that would continue to inspire me: Let the Legacy Begin!

About the Author

Rick Clendenen has always had a heart for others and his focus has been on relationships. Because of that, he began mentoring as a young man and has continued it throughout his life. Mentoring is a way of life for him in training others, as well as being willing to be mentored himself. He brings his knowledge of relationship building into this, his first novel. He has also authored three other books and has co-authored one.

Rick and his wife Debbie reside in Benton, Kentucky. Their son Richie and wife Jenny are parents of their grandson, Trey. Their daughter Renee and husband Landon are parents of their granddaughter, Kyndal.

Follow Rick Clendenen

www.rcminc.org

Rick Clendenen Ministries, Inc.
PO Box 287
Benton, KY 42025
www.rcminc.org

Made in the USA
Middletown, DE
22 October 2016